Autumn spotted a gunman crouched behind a nearby boulder. The front of his Glock was pointed at her.

A Glock? The man definitely wasn't a hunter.

She spotted a fourth man behind another tree. They all surrounded the campsite where Derek and his brother had set up.

They'd been waiting for Derek to return, hadn't they?

Another bullet came flying past, piercing a nearby tree.

"What are we going to do?" Derek whispered. "Can I help?"

"Just stay behind a tree and remain quiet," she said. "We don't want to make this too easy for them."

Sherlock let out a little whine, but Autumn shushed the dog.

The man fired again. This time the bullet split the wood only inches from her.

Autumn's heart raced. These men were out for blood.

Even if these men ran out of bullets, she and Derek were going to be outnumbered. They couldn't just wait here for that to happen.

She had to act—and now.

She turned, pulling her gun's trigger...

Christy Barritt's books have won a Daphne du Maurier Award for Excellence in Suspense and Mystery and have been twice nominated for an RT Reviewers' Choice Best Book Award. She's married to her Prince Charming, a man who thinks she's hilarious—but only when she's not trying to be. Christy is a self-proclaimed klutz, an avid music lover and a road trip aficionado. For more information, visit her website at christybarritt.com.

Books by Christy Barritt

Love Inspired Suspense

Visit the Author Profile page
at Harlequin.com for more titles.

MOUNTAIN SURVIVAL

CHRISTY BARRITT

LOVE INSPIRED SUSPENSE

INSPIRATIONAL ROMANCE

LOVE INSPIRED® SUSPENSE
INSPIRATIONAL ROMANCE

ISBN-13: 978-1-335-40506-7

Recycling programs for this product may not exist in your area.

Mountain Survival

This edition published by arrangement with Harlequin Books S.A.

For questions and comments about the quality of this book, please contact us at CustomerService@Harlequin.com.

Love Inspired
22 Adelaide St. West, 40th Floor
Toronto, Ontario M5H 4E3, Canada
www.Harlequin.com

Printed in U.S.A.

I will lift up mine eyes unto the hills, from whence cometh my help. My help cometh from the Lord, which made heaven and earth.
—Psalm 121:1–2

This book is dedicated to Rusty, the best Australian shepherd out there. Thanks for the inspiration, sweet pup!

ONE

"It's up to you, Sherlock," Autumn Mercer murmured as she knelt beside her dog. "You have to find her."

Sherlock barked, his tongue hanging from his mouth as he panted with excitement.

Autumn held a sweater belonging to one of her coworkers beneath her dog's nose. Sherlock sniffed it before sitting at attention and waiting patiently for her command. The dog was practically salivating to get to work.

Autumn paused a beat before saying, "Search!"

At once, Sherlock tugged at his leash and started toward the thick forest on the edge of the small, secluded parking lot.

The dog never looked as happy as when he had a job to do. The Australian shepherd, a red merle with striking blue eyes, was always a sight to behold. In the three years since Autumn had been training him for search and rescue missions, the canine had become like a family member.

She followed behind him, careful to track her steps so she could find her way back later. Every month, Autumn did these exercises with her dog so they could be prepared when needed.

Just last week, she and her team had to track down a missing fourteen-year-old who'd wandered away from his family on a camping trip. Sherlock had also helped with search and rescue missions involving the elderly, hikers who explored off the marked trail and once an entire family who'd gotten lost while geocaching.

Sherlock paused near a tree and sniffed. Then he veered to the left, deeper into the wilderness.

"Good job, boy," Autumn said. "Keep going."

Autumn pulled her jacket closer as she tramped between hemlock and oak trees. Even though it was October, a chill lingered in the air today. It didn't help that the sun was obscured behind gray clouds overhead. A massive storm system was coming this way, but she had at least two hours until it arrived. She planned to make the most of her time.

As Sherlock pulled her, she glanced around. The leaves on the trees around her were gorgeous. There was nothing like fall in Virginia's Blue Ridge Mountains. At least, in her estimation.

She had worked as a park ranger here at the George Washington National Forest for the past five years, and it was her dream job. She'd always been an outside girl, preferring to spend time with nature rather than people. Being out here made her feel peaceful, and peace was something hard to come by at times. Especially lately.

Before sadness could grip her, she turned her attention back to Sherlock.

"Careful, boy," she called.

The trail narrowed, and a steep drop-off on one side gave them only six inches of slippery rock to cross to get to where they were going. Sherlock had no problem, but Autumn tried to brace herself. Heights had never been her favorite, and the fifty-foot drop made her feel light-headed.

This part of the mountain was no place for a rookie. A gorge cut through the area, and the Meadow Brook River rushed the depths there. If one wasn't paying attention, they might lose their step on one of the cliffs or rock facings. It still amazed Autumn how many people tried to hike this terrain, even without the proper gear or experience.

Kevin used to love exploring this section of the national forest. He'd loved adventure—but only when safety precautions were taken first.

At the thought of him, Autumn's heart squeezed with grief. It was hard to believe he'd been gone for three years now. A heart attack had taken him from this earth but not from her memory. He would always be there with her.

His death was just one more reason she liked being out here. Everyone she'd ever loved was gone. Her parents had died in a car accident when she was a teenager. Then her husband had passed away.

All she had now was Sherlock. Autumn had found the dog on the side of the road as she traveled home from Kevin's funeral. The canine was like a godsend in her time of need.

Though Autumn had previously been a ranger, she and Sherlock had gotten their certification in search and rescue. Sherlock had been a natural and had become a valuable part of her team.

Autumn and Sherlock had been inseparable ever since.

"What do you smell, boy?" Autumn watched as the dog's nose remained close to the ground.

Sherlock continued to tug her through the trees. Autumn watched her steps, careful not to lose her footing on the slick leaves that lined the forest floor. As she moved, a chilly breeze swept over the landscape—a breeze that smelled like rain.

The storm was coming. Maybe it was even closer than forecasters had predicted. They didn't have a lot of time to waste. Thirty more minutes, and Autumn would head back to the Park Service SUV she'd left in the small lot off the windy mountain road. There was nothing else there but a portable toilet, a small display with a map and a wooden box for donations.

Sherlock continued to pull on his leash, leading her through the foliage. But Autumn's muscles pulled tighter across her back with every pace forward.

Steps sounded ahead of her. Twigs broke. Leaves crackled.

Autumn paused. Sherlock's tail straightened, and his hair rose.

Her hand went to her gun, and she braced herself, preparing for the worst.

She held her breath, waiting to see what creature might emerge from the trees in the distance. Whatever it was, it sounded big. A bear? She'd seen her fair share of the beasts out here. She liked admiring them, but only from a distance.

Sherlock let out a low growl.

A moment later, someone darted from the trees. A big man with broad shoulders and short dark hair. He wore jeans, a thick vest and a knit cap.

As soon as Autumn saw his face, she knew he wasn't trouble. Instead, he was *in* trouble.

Sherlock began barking at him, and the man froze. His breaths seemed shallow. Too shallow. His cheeks were flushed, and his gaze unsteady.

"Heel, boy," she told the dog. Caution lined her voice.

Sherlock quieted and waited for her instructions, but his eyes remained on the stranger. Autumn quickly studied the man. Just looking at him, she didn't see any visible injuries. But the look in his eyes told a different story.

"I'm Ranger Autumn Mercer," she called. "Can I help you?"

The man continued to heave with exertion. "I've been

trying to find help. It's my brother. He broke his leg, and I don't have any cell service out here. He needs help."

Based on the desperation in his eyes, the break had been bad. The man was clearly concerned.

Autumn glanced above her at the clouds that were becoming darker and darker by the moment. She didn't have much time to make her choice. She would radio for backup, she decided.

Then she would go and try to help the man herself.

Because if his broken leg wasn't dangerous enough, the approaching storm was.

Before the thought had time to fully develop, gunfire rang out in the distance.

Her back muscles tightened.

It appeared a trifecta of trouble had found them. Autumn braced herself for whatever waited ahead.

Derek Peterson's lungs tightened, and his gaze swerved to the park ranger's as the sound of someone shooting echoed across the mountains.

"It's probably hunters," she said, her voice as calm and steady as her gaze.

"I wasn't aware people hunted around here in October." He wasn't an outdoorsman himself, but he knew that the season didn't start until November.

"They're not supposed to, but that doesn't always stop them." Ranger Mercer plucked her radio from her belt. "I'll call it in, along with a request for help."

Derek found only slight comfort in her statement about the gunfire.

He'd never been so happy to see another living soul as he had when he spotted the ranger and her dog. He'd been rushing through the wilderness for what felt like hours. Trying to quickly navigate these mountains had been challenging, at best. As an attorney, he got his adrenaline rushes in the courtroom.

He observed the woman for a moment.

She almost looked too young to be a park ranger. She had auburn-colored hair that had been pulled back into a neat ponytail. Now that Derek thought about it, her hair and her dog's hair almost matched. Both were a lovely shade of a rusty red.

Ranger Mercer put her radio back on her belt. "Help is on the way, but they're probably thirty minutes out still."

"Thank you."

"Where's your brother?" Ranger Mercer asked as she began walking in the direction he'd emerged from. "I want to see him myself."

"We set up camp down by the river," Derek said. "We've been backpacking through the area for the past three days."

She nodded, but her features still looked tight. She was apprehensive about all of this also, wasn't she? Anyone in their right mind would be.

"How did he hurt his leg?" she asked.

Derek took a deep breath. He usually had an even disposition. He had to for his job as an attorney. Besides, all those years in JAG—the justice branch of the military, also known as the Judge Advocate Generals Corp—had trained him to stay cool under pressure. But seeing his brother hurt and having to leave him…it had Derek rattled.

"He was climbing up some rocks when he fell. His leg got caught between two boulders. He managed to get himself out, but his leg…it was torn up." His voice cracked as he remembered seeing the injury. "Just looking at it, the bone was obviously broken. He's in a lot of pain and can't walk."

Her expression remained even. "How long ago did this happen?"

"Probably an hour." Derek continued walking beside her through the forest. The woman seemed to know where she was going, and she kept a steady pace as she moved. Thank God he'd found her when he did. She was an answer to prayer, for sure.

"You did the right thing by coming to find me."

"That's good to hear, because I hated to leave him." Derek prayed that William was okay. Derek didn't see how a rescue helicopter could get down to the thickly wooded area. He had no idea how his brother would be rescued, considering there was no way William could walk right now.

"These mountains aren't for amateurs, that's for sure."

Derek frowned at her words. She was right. This trip had been tough, had made both Derek and William dig into their adventurous side. The slopes were steep and rocky. The area was lonely and not well traveled. Plus, the weather had been iffy.

"This trip was my brother's idea," Derek said, squeezing through the trees. "I was just trying to help him out. He had an especially bad breakup a couple months ago, and I think he needed to get away."

None of that really mattered anymore, did it? All that mattered was helping his brother. William had always been the troublemaker of the two.

He was younger than Derek by two years, and something about his little brother had always been rowdy. William had been the one in detention. The one who'd gotten into fistfights. Yet he'd also been the one who was the captain of the football team and homecoming king. Derek, on the other hand, was the responsible one. He'd played baseball, studied hard and worked part-time jobs to save money for college.

"What's your brother's name?" Ranger Mercer asked,

clucking her tongue at her dog as the leash pulled tight. The canine seemed eager to move ahead.

"William."

The ranger's dog continued to lead her through the wilderness, acting like he knew exactly where he was going. As they moved forward, he remembered the sound of bullets just a few minutes ago.

"Where are the two of you from?" Ranger Mercer asked.

"I'm from Washington, DC. I'm a lawyer there. My brother works in finance in New York City. We don't get together that often, but we both thought this trip might be good for us."

"Seems like an interesting choice of places to meet." She glanced back at him, as if trying to study his expression.

"My father used to take us camping and hiking in this area when we were boys."

"Sounds nice." Her voice softened.

"He passed away a couple years ago. We thought this could help us get some closure."

"I'm sorry to hear that."

Derek was also. It had been one of the most challenging times of his life. Only a year later, Derek's fiancée had left him at the altar.

To this day, Derek had a hard time trusting people. When the people you cared about the most let you down, whom could you put your faith in?

He still wasn't sure about the answer to that question.

They continued through the wilderness. Thankfully, Derek had a good sense of direction. Otherwise every path would look the same.

Finally, Derek heard the river in the background. In this section, the rapids skipped and hurried over large boulders. Not far from here was Beaver Falls, a one-hundred-foot waterfall. The rapids grew more turbulent as they inched closer to the drop-off.

Earlier, he'd thought the sound was soothing. Now it seemed a grim reminder of what had happened.

Thankfully, they were almost to the area where he'd left William. Thunder rumbled in the distance, and Derek knew he didn't have much time.

Even though the park ranger had called for backup, Derek knew that getting out to this area was going to be difficult for the rescue teams. It wasn't easily accessible, which was one of the reasons that he and William had wanted to come here.

No, Derek corrected. It was one of the reasons *William* had wanted to come here. Derek would've been just as happy hiking the Appalachian Trail or a path a little more well traveled.

"It's just ahead," he said.

"We should walk a little faster." Ranger Mercer glanced up and frowned.

Her expression seemed to confirm that this was a bad situation all around. The weather would not be their friend.

They quickened their pace, just as the wind began to pick up. Derek knew it was going to storm today. He and his brother had set up camp early because of it, knowing they'd need shelter.

"This is the tricky part," he called to the ranger. She probably already knew this area, but he felt inclined to say something anyway.

But they'd reached a ledge. They had to angle themselves through a small opening, walk along the side of a rock wall and then they'd eventually reach the riverbed. Normally people hooked up safety lines here, just in case they slipped. They didn't have time for that, though.

"Watch your step," she muttered.

Derek wasn't sure if she was talking to him or to her dog. Either way, they all needed to be careful.

They squeezed between the rocks and began the challenge of balancing themselves on the rocky cliff. As the ranger stepped in front of him, the rocks crumbled beneath her feet, and she started to slip.

Derek grabbed her arm and pulled her back up. Her wide eyes met his as she murmured, "Thank you."

"No problem."

They continued walking.

Derek hadn't anticipated any of this happening. A medical emergency while they were in the middle of nowhere. The strange thing was that he'd always been a planner. He liked to know what to anticipate. He didn't like surprises.

All of this was like a test. He knew they were going to get through it. He just dreaded the process.

"It should be right on the other side of this boulder." Derek pointed to the moss-covered rock ahead.

Ranger Mercer nodded and took the lead, her dog walking in front of her.

But just as they cleared the boulder, another sound rang out.

More gunshots.

"Get down!" Ranger Mercer yelled.

Derek ducked to the ground just as a bullet splintered the tree beside him.

What was going on?

One thing he knew for sure: those were not hunters.

They were killers.

TWO

As soon as the gunshots faded, Autumn reached for her holstered weapon. As a park ranger, she didn't have to use it often. But Kevin had taught her how to shoot, and she would defend herself, Sherlock and Derek, if she had to.

After another bullet whizzed by, she turned, trying to get a better view of the gunman. She had to figure out where he was.

"Stay behind the tree," she whispered to Derek. "And keep an eye on Sherlock."

She turned and scanned the landscape around her. Finally, she spotted a gunman crouched behind a nearby boulder. The front of his Glock was pointed at her.

A Glock? The man definitely wasn't a hunter.

Autumn already knew that, though.

Hunters didn't aim their guns at people.

Her gaze continued to scan the area. She spotted another man behind a tree and a third man behind another boulder.

Who were these guys? And what did they want from Autumn?

Backup couldn't get here soon enough.

The breeze picked up again, bringing another smattering of rain with it. They didn't have much time here. The conditions were going to become perilous at any minute.

The storm might drive the gunman away, but it would present other dangers in the process.

She spotted a fourth man behind another tree in the distance. They all surrounded the campsite where Derek and his brother had set up.

They'd been waiting for Derek to return, hadn't they?

Why? What sense did that make?

She didn't have time to think about that now. Another bullet came flying past, piercing a nearby tree. She heard Derek suck in a breath beside her.

As far as she could tell, only one of the men had a gun in his hand.

That was good news, at least. She'd take whatever she could get.

"What are we going to do?" Derek whispered. "Can I help?"

"Just stay behind a tree and remain quiet," she said. "We don't want to make this too easy for them."

Sherlock let out a little whine, but Autumn shushed the dog. He lowered his head.

The man fired again. This time the bullet split the wood only inches from her.

Autumn's heart raced. These men were out for blood.

Even if these men ran out of bullets, she and Derek were going to be outnumbered. They couldn't just wait here for that to happen.

She had to act—and now.

She turned, pulling the trigger.

A yelp sounded in the distance.

She pressed herself back into the tree, her breathing labored.

Had she just done that? Her head pounded.

She'd had no other choice. Their lives were on the line

right now. That still didn't stop the adrenaline—and some unnecessary guilt—from pounding through her.

Movement sounded behind her. What were the men doing now?

"I think they're leaving," Derek whispered, peering between two trees that practically hugged each other.

Surprise washed through her. Maybe they were taking their injured man back to their own camp to get him help. That's what she could hope, at least.

But it was too soon to leave their shelter. She had to know for sure that the men were gone.

Drawing in the last bit of her courage, she peered around the tree one more time. Just like Derek had said, the men scrambled in the opposite direction. One man had his arm around their injured comrade, and they walked away, occasionally glancing back.

"We'll come up with a new plan tonight," one of the men muttered.

It meant that they weren't done yet. These men would regroup, and they would come back.

That didn't leave her and Derek very much time to form a plan.

She waited several minutes until they were well out of sight. Then she turned to Derek.

"Stay here. I want to go double-check that they're gone before we continue."

"But—"

"Just wait here," she interrupted. This was no time for him to play the man card on her. She was a trained law enforcement officer, and she had to do her duty.

But she had to admit that a tremble claimed her as she stepped out, trying to brace herself for any danger that might emerge.

* * *

Derek's heart pounded into his chest. The last thing he wanted to do was to stand here while the park ranger investigated whatever had just happened. But were the gunmen really gone? What if they had just moved far enough away to keep an eye on them so they could draw fire again?

Dear Lord, please guard us. Be with William. Build a hedge of protection to keep us safe.

He knelt down beside Sherlock and rubbed the dog's head. "It's going to be okay, boy."

The canine let out a little whine, seeming just as worried as Derek felt.

Derek wished he had a weapon with him, but all he'd brought was a Swiss Army Knife. That didn't do much good in a gunfight, as the saying went.

But who would have thought all of this would happen? He certainly hadn't.

Derek waited, listening. He had to be sure that the men hadn't backtracked and come back this way. But he heard nothing but the wind and the rain. He was afraid the elements would obscure any sound of footsteps.

He squeezed his eyes shut and continued to pray that the ranger would be okay. That nobody else would be hurt.

And what about William? Where was he? Was his brother okay?

There were too many questions right now for Derek's comfort.

A moment later, Ranger Mercer appeared again, a frown on her face. "It's clear. For now. But we need to be quick."

He wasn't sure how to read in between the lines of what she was saying. But something was wrong. He was sure of it. Something the ranger didn't want to voice aloud.

Carefully, he climbed down the rocks toward the campsite he and his brother had set up near the river.

They needed to get William and get out of here. Hopefully, his brother had somehow managed to crawl out of sight and to safety. The best-case scenario was that he was hiding out here somewhere right now.

Derek wished he believed that was true. Another part of him knew better.

"William?" he called.

There was no response.

"Look over here." Autumn pointed to the ground in the distance.

Derek headed toward her and frowned. Blood smeared the dirt and rocks. A lot of blood.

"Was this here when you left?" The ranger's eyes crinkled with worry as she stared at him.

Derek shook his head, a throb beginning at his temples as worse-case scenarios played out in his mind. "No, it wasn't. William broke his leg, but there wasn't any blood."

Reality hit him. Something had definitely happened here in the time he was gone.

"I didn't see him with those men," the ranger said, as if reading his thoughts.

"Neither did I. But I don't know where he might be. The only other possibility that I can think of…" He couldn't finish the sentence.

Ranger Mercer squeezed his arm. "I'll look for him. But then we're going to need to take shelter." She glanced up at the dark clouds overhead. "We don't want to be out in this when that storm hits. It won't be safe for any of us. Okay?"

He nodded, but the throb remained at his temples. "Got it."

"Let's stay together," Ranger Mercer said. "I don't know what these guys are thinking, but I feel certain they're going to come back."

Derek followed Ranger Mercer's lead as she walked

around the perimeter of the site, examining everything she passed. Sherlock followed on her heels.

His—and his brother's—tent was still there, along with a little circle of rocks where they'd set up a haphazard campfire ring. Inside the tent, there should be William's backpack, as well as some water.

"I need you to grab something of your brother's." Ranger Mercer paused by the tent, looking like the consummate professional. "Maybe a shirt or some socks."

Derek nodded and hurried into the tent. His heart squeezed with worry as he remembered the carefree time he and William had shared just last night. They'd told stories about their childhood adventures. About fishing with their dad. About sneaking out at night. About taking their father's car for a test drive and being grounded for a month afterward.

How could things change so quickly?

Derek looked for his brother's backpack, but it was gone. Strange.

Had William grabbed it and then run?

He had no idea.

Instead, he grabbed a shirt that had been left beside the sleeping bag. This would work. He jammed it into his pocket before meeting the ranger again. She stood on a boulder, almost as if keeping lookout. The woman might be small, but she seemed formidable.

"We have to find shelter. Now." As soon as she said the words, the sky broke open. Water fell at capacity, it seemed, drenching them to the bone.

Sherlock barked, as if unhappy with the situation.

The ranger was right. It was no place to be during the storm. Between the cliffs and the slippery rocks, there was a little place for them to take shelter.

Even the tent he and his brother had set up would offer little protection in these elements.

They needed a plan. And they needed it now.

"Follow me," Autumn told Derek. "Stay close and watch your step."

The rain came down so fast that she could hardly keep the moisture out of her gaze. Water continued to soak into her eyes, making all of this even more difficult. Still, at least she'd been able to take some pictures to document the scene—just in case.

The only good news she could think of was that the weather might also prevent these guys from coming after them. But the rain also washed away any evidence that may have been left at the site.

The rain may have very well washed away William's trail also.

But they would have to worry about that later. Right now, they just needed to get to safety.

She searched her thoughts for places where they might take shelter. They need to get to high ground, but not too high. At the top of the mountain, the wind would be crazy. But in the valley, there was a chance of flooding.

Autumn knew this area almost like the back of her hand. At least, she thought she did. But there were thousands of acres within this parkland. It was impossible for someone to have explored all of it.

Despite that, Autumn kept moving forward. Maybe they could find a cave or a cove of trees that would offer them some shelter during the storm. Just as the thought crossed her mind, lightning flashed in the sky, followed by a loud clap of thunder.

The storm sounded so close that Autumn felt as if she

was a part of nature. The mountains even seemed to vibrate at the loud noise.

More lightning and thunder followed.

Then she heard a crack.

"Watch out!" Derek yelled.

His body collided with hers. They hit the ground.

As they did, a huge tree crashed beside them. Her foot was mere inches from the massive oak.

Sherlock…

She glanced ahead of her and released her breath.

There he was. Sitting on the trail, tail wagging as he stared at her.

Thank goodness he was okay.

They were *all* okay.

For now.

She shifted, realizing Derek's body was still covering hers.

He offered an apologetic smile before rolling onto his elbow. "Are you okay?"

His blue eyes stared at hers before he wiped his hands down his face, clearing the moisture.

"I am…fine. I think. Thank you."

"Of course."

She pushed herself to her feet and tried to pretend like her body didn't ache from where it hit the ground. Her mind reeled from being so close to this stranger. It made no sense.

"We should keep moving," she muttered.

Derek stood as well.

She glanced down. Mud covered her clothing, but she didn't care. They just had to move before another incident like that happened—only next time with worse results.

"There's only one place I can think of where we'll be safe," she yelled over the wind.

"I'm game for whatever plan you can come up with. I realize there probably aren't that many options out here."

The reality only made this situation more precarious. "No, there aren't. This place…it isn't too far away. I think we can make it before it gets too dark out here."

Derek nodded. "Let's keep moving, then."

It wasn't ideal, but it was going to have to work for now. Autumn felt better just knowing she finally had a plan.

They walked against the rain. The elements made each step feel like they were fighting twice as hard. The rain sloshed inside Autumn's shoes and soaked through her clothes.

They were going to need a fire to dry off or they'd both be sick.

As they reached a craggy part of the mountain, Sherlock barked beside her.

It was almost like the dog could read her mind and knew where she was headed.

She leaned toward him and rubbed his head. "That's right, boy. Let's go."

She followed Sherlock through the wilderness. They wound between trees and over rocks, all while the storm raged around them.

Finally, the rain let up a moment. Their steps slowed. Maybe they could catch their breath.

"The dog seems like a great wilderness guide," Derek said.

Autumn smiled at Sherlock. "He is. He loves it out here."

"So do you. At least, that's how it seems."

She shrugged. "I used to hate the great outdoors, believe it or not. But after working an office job for years, I knew something had to change."

"What did you do?" He pushed a branch out of the way as they continued climbing upward.

"I was an administrator for a health-care company." She pushed away the wet strands of hair that clung to her face.

"That's quite a career switch."

Up ahead, the dog easily climbed a boulder, taking a shortcut.

But Autumn's short legs were going to have a harder time with this.

"Come on, I'll help you." Derek scaled the boulder before reaching down to help her.

She hesitated before taking his hand. A moment later, he pulled, easily lifting her to where she needed to be.

For a moment, and just a moment, she lost her breath.

It was probably because of this whole experience. It was overwhelming, even for the most level-headed person. It had nothing to do with the man's firm grip or strong arms.

Collecting herself, she pulled away from Derek and tried to compose herself. What had gotten into her? It wasn't like her to react that way around practical strangers.

"Not much farther," she yelled over the wind.

They continued to follow Sherlock until he stopped in front of an old hunting cabin that had probably been on this land for a hundred years.

As soon as they climbed onto the porch, the pounding rain disappeared. A wave of relief rushed over Autumn.

Now she just needed to get inside and recalculate their next steps.

THREE

Derek glanced around the musty old cabin. It was dark in here, and the place looked like it hadn't been touched in years. Cobwebs hung in the corners, and dust seemed to cover everything.

But it was dry. Hopefully, they would be safe here for a while.

"I know it's not much, but it will do," Autumn said, her gaze scanning everything around them also. "For now."

"Do you think it's safe to make a fire?" Derek thought it was, but he would rely on her expertise since she was the professional here.

"It should be. I check on this place on occasion when I'm in the area. It's fairly well maintained. We're going to need to warm up, because the temperature is supposed to drop tonight. Besides, this rain is supposed to last for a while."

"I'll see what I can do to start that fire."

The ranger nodded. "I'll look for some candles or some light so we can actually see. The good news is I don't think these guys are going to chase us in this weather. It's going to buy us some time. Maybe my backup will be here by the time the storm ends."

"We can only hope," Derek said.

As she began to open and close doors and drawers in

the kitchen area, Derek went over to the stone fireplace. Some old wood had been left there. He arranged it, almost like a tent, with the kindling on the bottom and the larger logs on the top. Derek looked through a box beside it until he found a lighter. He tried a couple times until finally he had flame.

He would take whatever blessings he could get.

Carefully, he managed to start the fire. A few minutes later, a steady blaze crackled. He sat on the hearth for a minute, watching the flames and making sure it would keep. The warmth felt good.

"Pass me that light," the ranger said.

He did as she asked. A few minutes later, Ranger Mercer had candles and an oil lantern lit around the perimeter of the place.

Derek glanced around at the high wooden ceilings. It wasn't as bad here as Derek thought. In fact, if someone cleaned it up, the place wouldn't be that bad at all.

Two old couches sat along the walls, forming a living room area, and a small kitchen bumped up next to it. A loft stretched above them, probably with a bedroom or two. Around the corner, he'd guess there was a bathroom.

"It's a good thing you knew where this was." He glanced at the ranger as she studied the oil lantern another moment.

She turned away from the light as if she'd deemed it safe and paced toward him. "Yes, I am very thankful that I remembered it was here."

He looked down at Sherlock, who had lain beside him, probably trying to dry off near the fire. "And this dog seems to read your mind."

"Sometimes I feel like our wavelengths are connected."

She took her jacket off and sat beside him, rubbing her hands near the fire. She shivered, and Derek could see the goose bumps that popped out on her crossed arms.

"I have some dry clothes and socks you could wear," Derek offered.

"Actually, that sounds great. You should change, too."

A few minutes later, they'd both changed. Derek already felt better. They laid out their wet clothes to dry by the fire.

"Thank you," the ranger said.

"It's no problem, Ranger Mercer."

She glanced at him, something shifting in her gaze as she sat near the fire with him. "You know, why don't you just call me Autumn? We might be stuck together for a while. We might as well be on a first-name basis."

"Very well then, Autumn." He liked her first name. It fit with her red hair and freckles and natural beauty. She wasn't the type Derek envisioned wearing a lot of jewelry or makeup or fancy clothing. She didn't need to. Kind of like nature in the fall didn't need to do a single thing to make people's jaws drop.

A moment of silence stretched between them.

Finally, Derek cleared his throat. "What do you think happened to my brother?"

He saw the flash of concern on her face. "I don't know."

"Do you think those men took him?"

"It's hard to say." Autumn frowned. "If they took him, then where was he during the shootout? Did these men seek him out? Follow him? Or just stumble upon him?"

"I have no idea."

"If these men did have him, why did they wait around for you?"

"Again, I have no idea. But I can't stop thinking about the blood…" The words caught in his throat. "Could a wild animal have gotten to him?"

"I didn't see any animal prints close by. I don't think that's what happened."

"But he was bleeding…" Derek pressed his eyes closed,

unable to bear that memory and the what-ifs that accompanied it.

Autumn leaned forward again and squeezed his arm. "I know this is difficult for you. But we are going to do everything we can to get your brother back."

He nodded. But, inside, he knew there was much more to this than either of them could ever imagine.

Autumn felt an unusual compassion and connection with Derek. She'd been in plenty of situations where people were in distress. So she wasn't sure why this time felt different.

But when she looked into this man's eyes, she saw the sadness and the worry there. She wished she could take it away.

Just like she wished she could take away her own grief from losing her husband three years ago. But she wasn't sure that would ever fade. And if it did disappear, would guilt replace it? Guilt that she was no longer mourning the man she loved the way she thought he deserved to be mourned?

She shoved those questions aside. At least she could be thankful they had shelter and fire.

Instead, she glanced out the window. It was already getting dark outside. There was no way they should venture through these woods at night, especially in these conditions. Today had not turned out the way she envisioned.

The storm still raged outside. The winds slammed into the building, and Autumn could feel it practically swaying around them. Lightning electrified the sky, and thunder filled the air.

The conditions were treacherous on so many levels.

"Have you heard back from anyone?" Derek asked.

"Not yet," she said. "I wonder if the radio tower is down.

The good news is that my boss knows that I came out here. If I don't check in, they should send a team to check on me."

Even if the towers did come back up, she knew those gunmen could potentially listen in on anything she said through the airwaves. It would take a little bit of technical know-how, but it was possible. It made her hesitant to give out her location, even when she was finally able to reach somebody.

"How about a cell phone?" Derek asked. "Mine doesn't work but maybe yours does."

"There's no signal out here. I have my phone, but I just use it for pictures, mostly. It's not going to do us any good."

Derek felt Autumn's eyes on him, studying him. There was no need to beat around the bush here.

"What are you thinking?" Derek watched her expression. "I can see it all over your face. You're worried."

She leaned toward the fire, thankful for the warmth. "Like I said earlier, I think we will be safe here for a while, at least until the storm passes. Darkness is falling, my radio isn't working and the terrain around us isn't safe to travel on."

"So we wait here until morning?"

She nodded. "I think so. This isn't what I had planned, but we don't have much choice."

"And then?"

She considered his question a moment. The smart thing to say would be that they should go back to the parking lot where she'd left her SUV and wait for help. But she knew that Derek was anxious to find his brother.

And Autumn had the best opportunity to help him to do that. She'd seen where the man had last been. She had the man's shirt. And she had Sherlock, the best search and rescue dog around, as far as she was concerned.

But she couldn't do anything that would put Derek or Sherlock in danger. She desperately needed backup before they made any moves.

And, of course, all of that was provided they could even get off this mountain.

Would those men still come after them? Based on the look she'd seen in their gazes, the answer was yes. She didn't know what they wanted, but there was a vengeance in their eyes.

She studied Derek's face for a moment, trying to gather her thoughts. "Any idea why those men may have been at your campsite?"

"I have no idea." Derek swung his head back and forth, his gaze burdened. "Nobody else really knew that my brother and I were out here. The only thing that makes sense is that we happened to be in the wrong place at the wrong time. I heard some people talking at the café I stopped at in town before our hike. They said there are drug runners up in this area. Is that true?"

Autumn frowned at his words. She wanted to think of these mountains as a sanctuary. But that seemed impossible. There was always someone who wanted to abuse what could otherwise be perfect and beautiful. It seemed to be the nature of life.

"Any time you have a secluded stretch of land, there's a possibility that people might want to do illegal things there, out of sight from the rest of the world," she said. "So, to answer your question, yes, there are occasionally drugs that pass hands back here."

"So maybe William got scared, and he tried to find help himself," Derek said, one hand slicing against the other like a lawyer explaining something to a jury. "Instead of finding help, he ran across these guys, and they came back to see if he had left any money at the campsite."

"That's a good theory," Autumn said. "I'm just trying to figure out that blood we found."

Derek visibly flinched as she said the words. "I've been trying to figure that out as well. Do you have any ideas what it might be?"

She did have one idea, but she hesitated to say it out loud. She didn't want to burden Derek with opinions.

"Go ahead," Derek said. "I can handle it."

She let out a breath and leaned closer to the fire. "If these guys thought your brother had something they wanted, they may have resorted to violence in order to get answers. There's a possibility they pulled a gun on him, threatening him with harm if he didn't fess up to something."

Derek was a lawyer. Certainly, he had a firm grasp on the realities of criminal activities.

"Like where his money or car keys were?" he asked.

Autumn watched as the firelight flickered, softening his face. The look was nice on him, highlighting his strong profile. She looked away and breathed in the smoky scent of the fire, an aroma that brought an unusual amount of comfort.

If only there was any comfort to be found in this situation.

"Yes, something exactly like that," she finally said.

He let out a long breath. "My brother…he's a hedge fund manager. If somehow they found out about that…"

"Then he would be a perfect target," Autumn finished. "And it would explain why he's missing. Maybe these guys grabbed him so they could try to get some money out of him that way."

Derek hung his head, squeezing the skin between his eyes. "I just can't believe any of this. This trip was supposed to bring us closer together, to bring us healing."

She resisted the urge to reach out and touch him, to

offer him comfort. It seemed inappropriate, somehow. "I'm sorry. I know that life doesn't always work out the way we want it."

As soon as the words left Autumn's lips, she realized the truth in them.

No, her life certainly hadn't worked out the way she had wanted it to, either.

But now, more than ever, she wanted the opportunity to rebound, to find happiness again. Given her current circumstances, she wasn't one hundred percent sure that was going to happen.

There was too much on the line.

Mainly, her life.

Derek saw the emotion pass through Autumn's eyes. She understood pain, didn't she?

If he knew her better, he would ask her what she was thinking about. But he hardly knew the woman at all, though in some ways it felt like they had known each other years. What they had experienced today seemed surreal, and it had bonded them faster than normal.

But none of that mattered. Hopefully by tomorrow at this time, they would have found his brother and would all be on their merry ways.

He grabbed his backpack and pulled out some water. "Would you like some?"

"I have enough to last me and Sherlock tonight." She grabbed the small drawstring bag she'd brought with her and found the collapsible bowl she'd brought for Sherlock. Then she twisted the cap off and poured her dog some water.

Once the dog was happy, she took a long sip herself.

Derek tossed her a granola bar. "How about one of these?"

"That sounds great. I didn't realize how hungry I was." She would save part of this for the dog also. She had some treats for him, but they weren't enough to keep the dog satisfied for too long.

"You from around here?" Derek asked, figuring that question was safe enough.

"I grew up not far from here, in western Maryland. How about you? You said you live in DC now?"

"That's right. I grew up in Northern Virginia, though."

"You said you're a lawyer?"

"For a long time, I worked for the military. I was an attorney for JAG."

Her eyes brightened with curiosity. "Were you?"

"I just got out a couple years ago. It was okay. But it was time for me to move on. I can't say I regret it. Now I'm in private practice."

It had been hard to describe the feeling. He'd just known he needed a change. After Sarah had broken up with him, his life had felt out of balance.

He'd hoped the career change might bring clarity, but it hadn't. At least he was able to choose his cases now.

"Do you like being in private practice?" Autumn took a bite of her granola bar.

"It's what I've always wanted to do. My mom died when I was nine."

"I'm so sorry to hear that."

"She was in the wrong place at the wrong time. She went into the bank to deposit a check, and some men came into to rob it. She got caught in the crossfire. I knew after that happened that I wanted to do something to make sure guilty men and women got the justice they deserved."

"It makes sense. Do you and your brother go camping together often?" She stoked the fire.

"No, I can't say that. In fact, we've drifted apart over

the years. I thought this trip would be good for us. I had no idea I would be so wrong."

"I'm sorry to hear that." Autumn stood and walked toward the window.

Derek watched her, knowing exactly what she was doing. She was looking for any signs of trouble. They'd be foolish to let down their guard. He knew that also.

More thunder and lightning surrounded them. The sound seemed to echo across these mountains, making the noise seem even louder and stronger than normal.

Sherlock didn't seem to mind. He remained by the fire, seemingly content just to warm up.

"Is there anything I can do?" Derek asked. He hated how things had spun out of his control. Now he was at the mercy of nature, the mercy of this mountain and the mercy of this park ranger.

Autumn shook her head. "I don't know what to do except wait. I'll try my radio again, but I don't have much hope. Not with the storm going on."

Derek understood where she was coming from. Maybe once they both had time to dry off, they could figure out what they were going to do once they left this cabin.

Just as the thought entered his head, Sherlock let out a low growl.

Derek and Autumn's gazes met.

What did Sherlock hear that they didn't?

FOUR

Autumn knew what her dog's growl meant. Sherlock heard something. Probably outside the cabin, something that their human ears hadn't been able to pick up on.

Maybe those men were just brazen enough to come out in this weather to find them.

If that was the case, they must be really desperate for whatever it was that they wanted. She couldn't let on to how much that thought terrified her.

Autumn had to think quickly.

"Derek," she rushed, popping to her feet. "Can you lift up Sherlock and carry him up that ladder to the loft?"

His eyes narrowed with curiosity. "Sure, but what are you going to do?"

"I'll be up there in a moment. Just go."

He stared at her one more minute before nodding and lifting the dog up onto his shoulder. But he still seemed hesitant as he climbed the steps.

As soon as he did, Autumn hurried around the cabin and blew out the candles. She didn't have time to put the fire out, so it was going to have to stay. For now.

One last thing, she went to another door on the other side of the cabin and cracked it open.

She hoped her plan worked.

She grabbed her jacket and backpack before climbing up the ladder herself.

As soon as Autumn reached the top, she pulled the ladder up and out of sight. She leaned closer to Sherlock, who'd been standing near the edge, watching everything.

"Quiet, boy," she whispered.

After moment, the canine seemed to settle down.

She patted her hip. "Come on."

She, Derek and Sherlock quietly shuffled to the back wall, into the shadows there. The space was deep enough that no one should be able to see them—if they planned this right.

Would this work? Autumn didn't know. But she hoped so.

A moment later, voices drifted inside. She held Sherlock to her chest, praying he remained quiet. The dog was usually obedient, but she could feel the tension in his body. He knew danger was close and was poised to act.

The door screeched open, and footsteps sounded inside. Then more footsteps. And more.

Autumn exchanged a glance with Derek, and she saw the trepidation in his gaze as well. He knew how serious this was.

Had all four men come to see if they were here?

Autumn held her breath, praying for the best.

But she could feel the danger in the air.

After several minutes of listening to their footsteps, one of the men finally spoke. "They must have heard us coming and went out the back door. They must have left fast, because the fire's still going."

"What do you want us to do?"

"Let's search the surrounding area. They couldn't have gotten far."

"The only place in the cabin we haven't checked is up there."

Autumn pressed her eyes closed. If her plan worked, those men wouldn't be able to get up here. The loft was extra high. Hopefully these men would just think that the ladder had been lost.

Hopefully.

Autumn squeezed Sherlock harder, prayed more fervently.

"Maybe if we tip the couch on the side, we could lift somebody up there?" one of the men suggested.

"I suppose it's worth a shot, but I have a feeling they're long gone. Otherwise, why would the door be open?"

"Maybe we could torch the place," one of the men suggested.

Her breath caught. *Please, no...*

"It's a little wet outside for that, genius," one of the men said, the one who appeared to be the leader of the group.

Autumn heard something moving across the floor. Probably the couch. Those men were scooting it closer to the loft, weren't they?

But would her plan work? Even if they tilted the couch, how would they climb up it?

She heard a bang, and then one of the men let out a yell. "Rats. There are rats in this couch."

Scrambling and some cursing sounded below.

Maybe that would work in their favor.

"Let's start outside," that familiar voice said, the one who sounded like the leader. "We're wasting time in here. We can't let them get away."

The footsteps left the cabin.

Autumn looked at Derek and shook her head. They couldn't afford to move. Not yet. Not until they knew if these guys really were gone.

Even if the men were outside, that didn't mean that they weren't going to come back.

She probably had four more bullets in her gun. But she knew that these guys would not come back unprepared this time. She had to save that ammunition until she needed it the most.

Derek could hardly breathe. He'd been in plenty of sticky situations as an attorney, but none like this.

Thank goodness Sherlock was a good dog. Otherwise, the canine could have easily given away their location. One wrong move and…

Autumn put a finger to her lips, indicating they shouldn't move. His thoughts exactly. They couldn't risk anything giving away their presence, not until he knew for sure that these men were gone.

Thank goodness for Autumn's quick thinking when she'd left that door open. She'd probably saved their lives.

Derek stole a quick glance at her. Even though it was dark in the room, whenever lightning flashed outside, he caught a brief glimpse of her features.

He'd never felt such instant admiration for someone else. Autumn was not only smart, brave and strong, but she was also beautiful. The combination was enough to make his head spin.

Not that right now was the time to think about these things. But he needed *something* to think about, something other than the impending danger they were in.

Survival.

That's what he needed to think about. And, in order to survive, he needed to find answers.

His mind went back to William again. Where was his brother right now? Derek prayed fervently that his brother was alive and that he wasn't suffering too much. But between the broken leg and the bloodstains…

Worry gripped him.

He didn't even want to think about it. How had such a simple camping trip turned into this? It seemed nearly impossible, almost surreal. All of this seemed like a nightmare.

But it wasn't.

This was all too real.

Sherlock continued to sit alert beside them, the dog's intelligent eyes staring forward as if waiting for the command to attack. Autumn sat beside the dog and rubbed his back, occasionally whispering assurances into the canine's ears.

The two were quite a team, and Derek wondered what their story was. He wondered about the sadness in Autumn's eyes. He wondered about her life before this point.

But if he asked too many questions, she might also begin to ask him questions. Maybe it was best if they both kept their distance. Hopefully this would be over soon, and they'd both return to their normal lives.

Hopefully.

He listened. More thunder roared across the sky, just as loud as ever. The fire spilled light in the room in front of them, but the flames seemed to be dying. Along with that would be any warmth that it had offered.

Autumn and Derek remained in the shadows in the corner behind the bed. Out of sight from anyone who might be looking for them from above.

Certainly, those men were still out there. Still searching. If he and Autumn had tried to run, no doubt they would've been found and discovered. The terrain, the storm and those men were unrelenting.

But how were they going to get out of the situation?

What if the men didn't leave? What if they simply waited for Derek, Autumn and Sherlock to return? The three of them couldn't stay up here indefinitely.

That was when he heard more footsteps.

His heart rate quickened again.

The men were back. Their voices stretched upward.

"They got away," one of the men said. "I don't know how they did it, but I can't find them anywhere. And the rain is soaked through my clothing. I can't see anything, and I'm ready to call it quits."

"What did I tell you about quitting?"

There was that voice again. The voice of the man who was obviously the leader of the pack. He sounded meaner than the rest, harder.

But his voice was also missing the edge he'd expected. These men almost sounded cultured. They didn't strike him as drug runners.

Derek's curiosity grew even more.

"What do you want us to do now?" another voice asked.

"There's not much else we can do here. We can start tracking them again in the morning, as soon as the storm has passed."

The men didn't say anything for a minute. Finally, someone said, "You're right. Let's get back to the camp and check on our guy there. We don't want to leave him alone too long now, do we?"

Derek's heart lodged in his throat. Were they talking about William? It was the only thing that made sense.

His muscles bristled. They did have his brother, didn't they? The good news was at least William might still be alive.

"Okay, let's get back before it's too late," the leader barked. "First thing in the morning, we're searching again.

We're not going to stop until we find these guys and we get what we want."

Derek glanced at Autumn. That didn't sound good.

He had no idea what it was exactly that they wanted. Part of him didn't want to find out. But, for his brother's sake, he would have to.

Autumn released her breath. The men were gone. She was pretty sure this time they were really gone. But she still needed to be cautious.

That had been close. But she, Derek and Sherlock still weren't out of the woods yet.

"What do we do?" Derek whispered. "What do you think?"

That had been all Autumn had been able to think about. How she could get everyone out of this intact and un-scathed. She wished there was an easy answer, an easy solution, but there wasn't.

"I think we need to stay here for tonight," she finally said. "Up in the loft. Then, before sunrise, we can sneak out again and go for help. I'm hoping my radio will work by then."

Derek nodded slowly in agreement. "Who are those men? Do you have any idea?"

"None," Autumn said. "I was hoping you might. It sounds like they have your brother."

"That's what I thought, too." He let out a sigh and leaned back against the rough wood wall. "What a nightmare."

She could only imagine what he was going through right now. She wished she could do something to ease his pain, his anxiety. But she was in survival mode. She had to keep them alive and get them out of this situation.

Then she would think more about his brother.

"I know. And I'm sorry that you have to go through this." She rubbed her dog's head as she said the words.

"Does this happen often in your line of work?"

"Missing people? Yes. But a gang of gunmen chasing me through the woods while it's storming outside? No. Never."

He let out another sigh. "At least there's a little bit of warmth up here. And the storm may be passing."

"That is good news," Autumn said. "But there's a big weather system out there. I'm not sure we've seen the last of it, not if forecasters are correct."

She felt Derek studying her for a minute. She wanted to look away, but she didn't let herself. Was the man curious about her?

"How long have you and Sherlock been together?" he finally asked.

"Three years."

He leaned against the wall, an arm propped on his bent knee. "Did you always want to have a canine on the job?"

How much should Autumn say? The man seemed nice enough. And she had nothing but time to kill right now. Yet, at the same time, she valued her privacy. She didn't usually get personal with people while on the job.

"I actually found Sherlock on the side of the road when I was driving home from my husband's funeral," she finally said.

Derek's eyes widened. "I had no idea. I'm sorry to bring it up."

"It's okay. Sherlock just happened to be in the right place at the right time. I couldn't find his owner, and nobody claimed him, so I decided he could stay with me."

"Sounds nice."

"He seemed to have a knack for finding things, so I started training him for search and rescue. He was a natural. We've been best friends since then." She rubbed the dog's head, and the canine leaned into her.

"It does sound like he found you at just the right time, doesn't it?"

They exchanged a glance, and Autumn felt her cheeks heat as she realized she'd allowed herself to become vulnerable with this man she didn't even know.

"Yes, you're right." Her throat burned as she said the words. "Sherlock has been a real lifesaver, in more than one sense."

Derek still studied her face. "If you don't mind me asking, how long were you and your husband married?"

"Only a year and a half. He was jogging one day and had a heart attack. He hadn't had any problems until that point. The doctor just said it was a fluke." As Autumn said the words, numbness filled her. For so long, the pain had been fresh. With time, the shock factor had worn off as reality set in.

"It's hard. I can't imagine."

She glanced at his hand, ready to turn the attention away from herself. "Are you married? I don't see a ring, but not everybody wears one."

"No, I'm not. I was engaged, but my fiancée broke things off."

"That stinks," Autumn said. "I'm so sorry to hear that."

"So am I. But everything happens for the best, right? That's what you've got to believe in this kind of situation." He sounded like he believed the words, like he'd lived them.

Autumn had to admire that.

"You have no choice but to move forward, so you have to look for the best in it, I suppose," Autumn said. "Even in this situation."

Could good come from these dire moments? Every obstacle was the opportunity to draw closer to God. That was the case now as well.

"Yes, I suppose even in this situation," Derek echoed.

The two of them shared a glance.

She felt like she'd known this man much longer than she had. Sharing the same belief system could do that. She was grateful to be stuck with someone like Derek.

She shifted her thoughts back to survival, though.

"How about if I take the other side of the loft and you can stay here?" Autumn said. "We should get a little bit of shut-eye for now. Don't you think?"

"Seems like a good idea." Derek drew in a deep breath. "Thank you for everything you did for me today, Autumn. You too, Sherlock."

Autumn offered a smile. Derek was pleasant to talk to. Surprisingly so. But she needed to be careful and not open herself up too much. It wouldn't be wise.

Besides, she was going to need all the energy she could afford tomorrow if she wanted to get them out of this situation alive.

FIVE

Derek couldn't sleep. He'd found some old blankets in a trunk up in the loft and had laid them out on opposite sides of the room, well out of sight of anyone who might come back into the cabin. They were fairly clean, all things considered.

His lack of sleep wasn't because he wasn't comfortable. It wasn't even because he was cold.

It was because his mind wouldn't settle.

It felt unfair that he might rest when he had no idea what his brother might be going through.

That was what it all boiled down to.

Derek let out a sigh.

He couldn't see Autumn across the room, but he would guess she wasn't sleeping, either. Too much was on the line right now.

They could both feel it.

Danger seemed to tinge the air.

Finally, his watch showed that it was 4:00 a.m. Autumn must have been watching the time as well, because he heard her sigh. A minute later, little doggy footsteps clicked across the wooden floor toward him, and Sherlock greeted him with a wet nose.

He rubbed the dog's head, finding strange comfort in the

canine. He'd always wanted a dog, but his old job hadn't allowed him to get one. He'd worked too many late hours.

Maybe that would change when all of this was over.

"Good morning." Autumn ran a hand through her hair as she stood on the other side of the room. "Did you get any rest?"

His heart lodged in his throat. Something about the way she looked right now did something strange to his pulse. She seemed younger, more vulnerable. The look made her seem more human and less superhero.

Then again, maybe these odd circumstances were doing something to his mind. He felt an unusual connection with the woman. It would be the same for anyone in this situation, he felt sure.

He remembered her question. *Did you get any rest?*

"Not really," he finally said, stretching out his back. "How about you? Did you sleep any?"

"No. I had too much on my mind."

"I understand."

She held up a map in her hands. She'd obviously been looking at it, planning today's escape.

"I'd like to get a head start back before the sun comes up," she started. "We need to make sure the men don't head back this way."

"Understood," he said. "I'd prefer to get out of here before those guys decide to come back as well."

Derek dreaded thinking about running into those men again. He had a feeling that would be unavoidable, however. If he wanted to get his brother back, he didn't see how that would happen without a confrontation.

As Autumn started to lower the ladder down to the floor, he crossed the space and helped her. She started to go down, but he touched her arm, stopping her.

"Let me," he said. "I'd like to check things out first."

"I don't mind—"

"No, really, let me."

She stared at him another moment before nodding. "Okay, then."

Derek had gotten them into this mess. He preferred to be the one on the front lines in case something happened right now. It didn't matter if this was her job or not. He felt responsible for them right now. Even the park ranger needed someone to watch out for her.

Carefully, he climbed down, trying not to make any unnecessary noise. As he reached the floor, he glanced around.

He saw nothing and no one.

The cabin looked just as they'd left it last night, other than the couch that had been turned on its side.

But just because he didn't see trouble, it didn't mean they were safe.

Derek didn't know much about these guys, but he wouldn't put it past them to have somebody staked out outside, just waiting for any sign of movements. Those men struck him as that type.

He'd dealt with plenty of dangerous criminals in his job as a lawyer. Just never while he was this isolated in the wilderness. The legal system was usually his battlefield. It seemed much safer right now than their current situation.

He remained on the edge of the room, moving quietly. As he reached the window, he peered out.

Darkness stared back. Of course. He wasn't sure what he had expected.

He grabbed a fire poker and held it in his hands as he opened the door. At least it would be something to defend himself with, if he needed it.

As he stepped out, the old deck creaked under his feet.

Nature seemed to grow quiet around him, as if it sensed his presence and waited for his next move.

The outside still smelled like the storm—heavy rain and damp leaves. Occasionally, he heard random drops tapping against the foliage on the ground, the moisture falling from the leaves above. The wind was brisk outside, and the temperature was probably twenty degrees cooler right now than it had been yesterday. Thankfully, his clothes had dried off last night.

Carefully, he walked along the deck, listening for any strange sounds. His gaze scanned the dark woods for any out-of-place movements.

He saw nothing. No one made any moves.

Relief washed through him. That was a good sign.

He continued around the deck, which stretched around the entire house. After he'd been around the whole place twice, he went back inside. If there was anyone out there, they were still hiding and weren't triggered into action by his presence.

Derek hoped that was a good sign.

He looked back up into the loft and called, "I didn't see anybody. And it's not raining, but it is cool outside."

Autumn poked her head over the side and nodded. "Great. Can you help lower Sherlock?"

"Of course." He scaled the rickety ladder and took the dog into his arms. Carefully, he climbed down and set the canine on the floor. Sherlock shook off, almost as if the dog had too much pride to be manhandled like that.

Derek couldn't blame the beast.

As Autumn climbed down, he waited at the bottom, just in case she needed a hand.

Halfway down, one of the rungs broke. She began toppling backward.

Before she hit the ground, Derek reached out. She landed with an *oomph* in his arms.

Her nervous gaze fluttered up to him, and she said nothing for a moment. Instead, they stared at each other, some type of understanding passing between them.

Finally, Derek lowered her back to her feet.

Autumn brushed herself off, obviously flustered. "Thank you. Again. First the boulder and now this."

"No problem. I'm glad I was here to help."

Was that a rush of attraction he felt toward her? Had she noticed also? Sure, the woman was beautiful. But that didn't mean Derek was looking for any sort of romance right now. He had a feeling that Autumn would say the same.

Derek mentally brushed himself off and nodded. "I guess we should get going."

Autumn nodded and rubbed her throat, almost as if she'd felt it, too. "Let's go."

Autumn couldn't seem to get herself together. She attributed it to the fact that the rung on the ladder had broken just as she had stepped on it. That had to be it.

Her jitters had nothing to do with the fact that Derek had caught her. That she caught a whiff of his aftershave. That she'd felt his strong arms.

Was it possible that he could still smell that amazing after all this time in the rain and in the wilderness? She didn't know, but she definitely picked up on his piney scent. And she liked it, whether she wanted to or not.

She cleared her throat, hating the fact that she felt at odds with herself.

"Sherlock will alert us if anybody's hiding and just waiting for us to go past," she said. "If my calculations are correct, the parking lot should take us about an hour to hike back to. My SUV is still there, so we can go for help."

She pulled out her map and showed him their intended route.

"Did you try your radio again this morning?"

She nodded. "I did while you were out. There's still no signal. The towers must have gotten knocked out in the storm. It's the only thing that makes sense."

"The cold front really did some damage, didn't it?"

"It did. I'm nervous about what might be in store for today as well. We're going to need to watch our steps. If either of us gets hurt, I'm not sure we'll ever get back. We can't risk that."

As she said the words, something changed on Derek's face. Maybe reality had been driven home. Maybe he felt more determination than ever.

She didn't know.

They walked toward the door. Before they stepped outside, Derek grabbed her arm to stop her from exiting.

"Look, Autumn," he started. "I really appreciate all the help you've given me, and I'm really sorry that I got you in this situation in the first place. Truly. But I can't go back to the parking lot with you."

Certainly, she hadn't heard him correctly. "What do you mean?"

"I have to find my brother. I can't leave him out there with these men. I have to help him."

"That's exactly what we're trying to do—help him. I just need backup to make it happen."

Derek shook his head. "I'm not sure we have time to get that help. If William is hurt, time is of the essence. I need to get to him now."

Certainly, he wasn't thinking this through. If he was,

he'd see the error of his way. There was no good outcome to them confronting those men.

She had to talk some sense into him. "What are you going to do if you do find him? How are you going to help him then?"

He shrugged. "I don't know. I haven't thought all of this through. However, he needs me, and I can't let him down."

Autumn touched his arm, trying to break through to him. "Derek, there's no way you can take on four gunmen by yourself. You're foolish if you think you can. The only thing you're going to do is get yourself killed also." She needed to get through to him before he did something he regretted.

"I know it might sound foolish. I'm usually someone who likes a plan. But what if backup isn't coming? What if we can't get out of this area? Then what? Then we just lost an hour, and we're going to have to come back out this way anyway."

Autumn let him get his questions out. It was only fair to let him voice the thoughts aloud. But she wasn't sure what he was getting at.

Derek shifted. "Look, I'm not asking that you come with me. I don't want to put you or Sherlock in danger. I'm just saying that I won't be able to live with myself if I walk away right now."

Autumn stared up at Derek, not sure if she admired his stance or if she should shake him. But she supposed if she had a sibling or a loved one in the situation, she would do the same. At least she had a gun with her.

The weapon would help them, for a while, at least. And Derek did have a good point about the roads. If they were washed out, which Autumn suspected they were, then going back to the parking lot would serve no good except to get them to a vehicle.

"You don't even know where you're going, do you?" Autumn asked.

The man might be a great attorney, but he didn't seem like the type who could navigate this forest like she could. She knew this land—she'd experienced it. Derek was strong and capable, but it still wasn't safe to send him out alone.

"I was hoping you might point me in the right direction before you left." He stared at her, his gaze intense yet humble. His blue eyes were warm and intelligent. The start of a beard shadowed his face, and his hair was just short enough that it didn't have to be styled.

She hid her smile. "Even if I pointed you in the right direction, you probably wouldn't find your way back to your old campsite. No offense."

"No offense taken," he said.

Autumn had to make a choice. She knew what the right thing to do was. She had to help him. She just hoped that they didn't both end up dead.

"Come on," she said. "I'll take you where you need to go."

He tilted his head. "Are you sure?"

"I'm sure. But if I'm going with you, then we're going to have to set some ground rules. One of those is that we have to be smart here. No sudden moves. No trying to be a hero. We simply try to find your brother and continue to try to get help. Understand?"

He nodded, gratitude evidence in his rolling voice. "I understand. And thank you."

Though Derek didn't want Autumn to put herself in danger, he was grateful that she and Sherlock were there to help him navigate this wilderness. Truthfully, this was the type of place a person might get lost and never be found.

The place seemed vast and overwhelming. He had chosen to use his time at law school studying rather than out in nature. Right now, that seemed like a mistake.

Autumn turned her flashlight on and aimed it at the damp ground. Footprints had been left in the mud there. "What do you say we try to follow these tracks and see where the men went?"

"I think that seems like a great idea."

She leaned down and said something to Sherlock. He barked back at her. Then the dog took off ahead of them, pulling at the leash.

Derek and Autumn followed. As they moved, Derek's senses remained on alert as he waited for any surprises. He knew that those gunmen weren't the only dangerous thing out here. There were also wild animals and hazardous cliffs, not to mention the mudslides and the flooding. So much could go wrong.

He briefly squeezed his eyes shut and lifted a prayer. *Dear Lord, please watch over us right now. Keep us safe. Be with William also. He needs you in more than one way. Protect him. Please.*

They continued to follow those footsteps. Sherlock was a great dog, so intelligent and so good at doing this. It was one of Derek's first times seeing a working dog like this, and he was impressed.

He and Autumn didn't talk as they walked. It was better if they stayed quiet, he figured. Just in case anyone was out there watching or listening.

Not far into their trek, Autumn paused in front of him and raised her hand back to stop him. He leaned over her shoulder, trying to see what was going on.

As she shined her light down on the ground, he saw a little stream.

"This isn't an actual creek, but runoff from the rainwater," she told him. "We need to be careful when crossing this."

Sherlock looked back at them before sniffing in circles.

"What's the dog saying?" Derek asked, certain that something was wrong.

"He lost the trail and he's trying to find it again."

Derek's pulse pounded in his ears as he tried not to lose hope. "Is that unusual?"

"No, it's not. Especially not with the rain like it is. Sherlock is a good search and rescue dog, but he has limitations. I have a feeling this runoff may have covered the trail."

"And if it did?" What did that mean for them finding William? Derek couldn't stop the question from echoing in his mind.

"If that is the case, then we are going to need to recalculate."

He didn't like the sound of that. Everything seemed to be going so well. They'd appeared to be on track to possibly find William. In Derek's mind, there was a chance that they might even arrive at these men's campsite before the sun rose and surprise them.

Now it looked like it wasn't going to happen.

"Can't we just follow the runoff?" Derek asked.

Autumn continued to stare ahead. "It's not safe. It's slippery, and that water is stronger than you might think it is. Plus, with all the drop-offs around us…it could be a death wish."

"What do you suggest that we do?"

She looked up and to the side, as if using her experience to calculate their next step. "If we have lost their trail, then it's going to be hard to figure out exactly where they are. We could wander around out here for days and not find these men. We need to have an idea of where they might be first."

"I agree." What she said made sense.

"The only other thing that I can think of is that we go back to your campsite and see if we can pick up a trail there. It's also going to be difficult, though."

"Doing something sounds better than doing nothing."

Autumn's eyes met his. "There's a good chance that your campsite is completely gone by now, too. I just want to warn you of that."

Derek flinched at her words, even though he knew that they could be true. "It's still worth a try, right?"

She stared at him another moment, almost as if ascertaining that he understood the implications of doing that. He must have passed her test, because she nodded. "Okay, then. Let's do it."

"You know how to get there?"

"I can find my way there. I know it was located to the east. And the sun's going to be coming up soon, so we can follow that. Like I said before, though, we're just going to need to be careful and watch our steps. This is dangerous terrain, even for the most skilled hiker."

Derek was beginning to feel more and more confident that coming across Autumn was an answer to a prayer he didn't even know he had muttered.

But they were far from being out of danger. No, if anything, the worst was yet to come.

SIX

Just as the sun began to rise, filling the sky with a touch of muted oranges and blues, Autumn heard the river rushing in the distance.

Except she shouldn't hear it.

That meant that the banks were overflowing.

Just as she had expected...or feared.

If the banks had spilled over, it was going to be nearly impossible for the three of them to follow these men's trails. She wanted to do what she could to help Derek.

She knew how much his brother meant to him. But another part of her felt like maybe they were wasting their time and needlessly putting themselves in danger. The pull inside her stretched tighter, the tension undeniable.

If only her radio would work, all of their problems would be over. Maybe not *all* of their problems, but a good portion of them. She'd tried it again this morning, but it still wasn't working.

She hoped that Derek didn't get his hopes up too high. The chances that they were going to find William and that he was going to be okay were slim. But she didn't dare to say that out loud. Derek had already been through a lot. She could only imagine the worry that he must feel.

He was a pleasant companion. He wasn't too pushy, nor

did he seem to feel like he had to be macho in front of her. She appreciated those qualities.

There were definitely worse people she could be stuck out here with.

As the wind swept over them again, bringing a chill with it, she smelled the incoming rain. They were far from being out of the woods—both literally and figuratively. She tried not to worry what the rest of the day might bring, but she had a feeling it would be treacherous.

"Are we close?" Derek asked.

"We're less than a mile away," Autumn said. "I'm hoping we can find some answers once we get to the campsite. I wish we'd looked for your brother's backpack more while we were there yesterday. If I knew then what I know now…"

"I looked earlier but didn't see it. I'm not sure what happened to it. You think there's some kind of clue inside?"

"He probably had some supplies, for starters. Maybe there was even a clue inside as to why all this happened."

"You mean all this may not have been random?" Derek's steps slowed.

"That's a possibility worth exploring, at least."

"I'm not sure I understand."

Autumn swallowed hard, choosing her words carefully. "I'm just saying that those men sounded relatively smart, and the clothes they're wearing are expensive. I don't think they're the type to just hang out in the woods looking for victims. What if somebody followed you and your brother out here?"

"Why would they do that?" Disbelief stretched through his voice.

"You're the only one who can answer that. Or maybe I should say, your brother is." She glanced behind her and offered a compassionate smile. She knew this conversation couldn't be fun.

"I… I just don't know. I don't want to think about William being mixed up in anything that's bad news."

"I understand that. But we need to be open to other possibilities right now."

She glanced behind her again just in time to see Derek frown. She knew it wasn't easy to hear, but the smart thing was just to share that news with him.

"You're really good with this, you know." He moved a branch out of their way as they continued to hike.

"My husband was also a ranger, and he was an avid outdoorsman. He taught me a lot."

"He sounds like quite a guy."

"He was. I still have trouble believing that he's gone." Autumn's heart panged as she said the words. She hadn't intended on saying them aloud, but she had. She didn't talk about her grief often.

"Losing the people we love is always difficult. I don't know what you believe, but I'm always grateful to know that we'll see them again one day, if they were believers."

His words washed over her. Derek was a Christian, too, it sounded like. "I believe that with all my heart. Prayer and faith are the only things that have gotten me through the past couple years."

He offered a soft smile. "I understand."

Something about the moment made her bond with this stranger feel even stronger. She couldn't explain it, nor did she want to. But the fact that they shared the same faith would get them far. They were going to have to rely on forces far stronger than themselves if they wanted to survive.

Dear Lord, please be with us now. Give us wisdom. Guide our steps. Protect us from our enemies. Keep us safe from nature.

She had so many prayer requests. If they got out of this situation alive, it would only be by God's grace.

Not much farther, and they should be there.

But as they skirted around a boulder, she heard a strange sound and froze.

All of her senses went on alert.

Trouble was close.

She was certain of it.

As if to confirm it, Sherlock began to growl.

Derek felt Autumn bristle in front of him.

Something was wrong, and Sherlock confirmed it. The hair on the dog's back rose, and his tail shot up ramrod straight.

Autumn's hand reached out, stopping Derek in his tracks.

Derek didn't dare to speak. He knew better than to make a sound. Derek glanced around, looking for the source of her distress.

He saw nothing.

Then why did it feel like they were being hunted?

Autumn put a finger to her lips, indicating for him to remain quiet. Then she began creeping forward, tugging on Sherlock's leash so he wouldn't get too far ahead.

Was it a wild animal? The gunmen? Or something else completely?

He didn't know.

But he could hear the river raging in the background.

Yes, raging.

The river wasn't normally like that. It had been perfect for fly-fishing and wading just yesterday morning. Derek was anxious to see exactly what it looked like now. Would it be one more obstacle for them?

Instead of walking straight on the path they'd been on,

Autumn began climbing over some boulders. This route would definitely be more perilous, but she had to have a good reason for it.

Derek trusted her—and he hardly ever trusted anyone. As a lawyer, he'd seen too many good people ruined because they'd trusted the wrong person.

He climbed behind her, watching her carefully, not wanting a replay of his brother's accident.

Every time he thought about it, he cringed. Hearing his brother's leg snap as it had been caught between two boulders…it was something Derek wasn't likely to ever forget.

Even thinking of it now reminded Derek of how much danger his brother was in, with or without those gunmen chasing them. If there was one thing their father had taught them, it was that they always needed to have each other's backs. *That's what family is for*, his dad always said.

Those wilderness trips with their father had made a big impact on Derek. But now this area might be forever tainted in his mind.

They continued to climb across the boulders, and Derek imagined how the large rocks had gotten here, all crashed together in one area.

Again, it just showed the power of nature. It could be a beautiful but formidable foe.

His nerves grew tense at the thought.

You had to respect nature, because you never knew what might happen next.

As if in affirmation, the sun disappeared and dark clouds moved overhead. Thunder rumbled in the distance.

They were in for another storm. That meant they needed to move even more quickly. They couldn't afford to be caught out here again. The results this time might not be as good as they had been before.

Should they try to make it back to the cabin? Or was Autumn's car closer and safer?

He had a lot of questions but no real answers.

Autumn paused and put her finger to her lips again. She crouched down and peered over a boulder, making sure that Sherlock was secure beside her.

As she did, a new sound filtered through the air.

A shout, followed by the sound of a bullet slicing the air.

It was the gunmen.

They were here.

And they had spotted them.

"They have us surrounded!" Autumn ducked down low, pulling Derek with her. She put an arm around Sherlock, making sure the dog was sheltered and safe.

"They must have seen us coming," Derek muttered, squatting down beside her.

"I agree. They were waiting here for us. I'm not sure why, but we'll have to figure that out at a different time."

He stared at her, his gaze intense. "How are we going to get out of this? Do you have any ideas?"

Autumn glanced around, her mind racing. There was only one direction where the men weren't located.

Behind them.

Where the river was located.

But the dangerous, raging river had rapids that would pull them downstream until they hit Beaver Falls. If they went down the one-hundred-foot waterfall, they wouldn't survive. She was certain of that. But they had very little choice here as to what they could do.

An idea hit her.

"Do you have a good balance?" she asked Derek.

"Not bad. Why?"

"I'm going to need you to follow me. And I'm going to need you to trust me." Autumn waited for his response.

Derek nodded. "Okay, then."

"This way, and stay low," she instructed.

Moving carefully, she maneuvered between the boulders. As she reached the other side, she paused and sucked in a deep breath.

There was the river. It looked even worse than she had thought it might. Not only were the banks swollen, the land around them seemed to be drowning. To make matters worse, the rocks were slippery, and the thunder above them was getting closer.

The timing couldn't be worse.

Despite that, Autumn knew what she had to do. It was the only choice if they want to survive right now.

But who knew if these men were going to back off? In fact, if Autumn wasn't careful, these guys would follow them. That meant they need to move quickly but efficiently.

Autumn rounded one more boulder, this one close to the river. She looked down. It was at least a fifteen-foot drop down into the water below. But it wasn't just water. It was rocky water. Her body would shatter on those stones.

She shuddered.

Thankfully, Sherlock was great with heights and had no problem walking along the ledges there.

There was no way she would ever endure doing this unless in a dire situation.

A situation like this.

She looked ahead and saw the ledge there. Derek seemed to follow her gaze.

"You're kidding, right?" Derek asked.

"I wish I was. But the ledge is about four inches. If we're careful, we can make it."

"But there's nowhere for us to hide if these guys come after us. We're easy targets."

Her gaze met his. "I have a plan for that. Like I said, you just have to trust me."

Finally, Derek nodded and began inching along behind her on the ledge. As Autumn took another step, the rock beneath her feet crumbled. She pressed herself into the rock wall and caught her breath.

Her heart pounded out of control.

Derek exchanged a quick look with Autumn, and he nodded at her again. She continued edging along the wall. By her estimations, she only had another twenty feet until she reached the area where she needed to go.

But if she didn't time this just right, the gunmen would find them before that.

She resisted the urge to close her eyes.

She couldn't let her fear of heights hinder her.

She had to keep moving, to focus on her goal and not her obstacles.

Dear Lord, help us now. We need You more than ever.

Slowly and surely, they made progress, getting closer to the area that could ultimately be their safe haven. Autumn felt certain that these men did not know about her destination. Unless they were regulars in the area, they would have no way of realizing this place was there.

The only reason Autumn knew about this area was because some college students had been stuck here after drinking too much and then taking a hike. Their judgment had been impaired, to say the least. There'd been an emergency rescue in order to get them out, and Sherlock and Autumn were a part of it.

"They're behind us," Derek whispered.

Her heart leaped into her throat. She glanced behind her just in time to see the men on the rocky ledge.

"You might as well stop running!" one of the men yelled. "We're not going to give up."

"Just keep walking," Autumn muttered, ignoring them. They only wanted to incite fear. She couldn't let them win.

"How much farther?" Derek's eyes were wide with anticipation.

But the gunmen weren't as careful as they were. That meant they were moving faster and gaining time on them. She had to resist the urge to move too fast herself and do something careless.

Sherlock's hind legs began to slip, and he let out a whine. Autumn grabbed the leash to hold him up. As she did, Derek reached down and grabbed the canine's hind legs, planting them firmly back on the ledge.

Relief filled her. She couldn't handle anything happening to her dog. This canine had been her sanity for the past three years, and finding him had been like a gift from God Himself.

Another bullet pierced the air, hitting the rock beside her.

Autumn's heart pounded faster.

She couldn't get to the secure location fast enough.

Because men were gaining on them.

And if they saw where they went…

Autumn shook her head. She couldn't think like that. She just needed to keep moving, to keep her eyes on the goal.

Just then a yell sounded behind her, followed by a tumble of rocks.

She glanced back just in time to see one of the men tumble down the cliff and into the water.

SEVEN

Derek heard the commotion behind him. He looked over in time to see one of the gunmen slide down the rocky cliff.

"No!" the man yelled, his arms flailing.

Derek held his breath as he watched the man hit the water. Immediately, his body was swept downstream in the turbulent rapids. The river pulled him under, making it clear he didn't stand a chance.

"Dear Lord…" Derek muttered the prayer, unsure what else to say, to do.

"We have to keep moving," Autumn said.

Derek glanced at her and noticed that her face looked paler. He had a feeling she was the type who'd stop to help, even if these men were the bad guys.

But not in this situation. In this situation, these guys would kill them.

Maybe they had even more reason for their vengeance now.

One of the gunmen shouted, and all of them began scrambling to try to rescue their friend. They attempted to climb down the rocks.

If they weren't careful, someone else was going to be swept away.

Derek pulled his gaze back to Autumn. She nodded in

the opposite direction, reminding him that they needed to keep moving.

That was right. They had no time to lose.

He looked back one last time as the men attempted the rescue.

His heart panged with regret.

The man who'd fallen into the river was now gone, out of sight. His friends continued to climb downward.

Derek knew enough to realize there was no hope.

He, Autumn and Sherlock kept moving.

He had no idea where Autumn was taking him, and he had no choice but to trust her. She hadn't let him down yet.

Several steps later, the cliff ended.

At least, Derek thought it did.

But as Autumn continued moving, he realized it was actually a corner. Autumn carefully skirted around it, staying close to the cliff wall.

He held his breath as he watched the dangerous move.

His lungs deflated when he saw her make it to the other side.

Autumn was okay.

Thank God.

The incident that had just happened with the man behind him had driven home reality. They were in a place where one mistake could cost them their lives.

Derek followed her lead.

After this, he'd have no urge to go rock climbing again. He had gotten his rush of adrenaline for a lifetime on this trip.

As the river wall shifted, Autumn climbed onto a boulder. They were still high up. A safe distance from the water. But she nodded for him to follow her lead, and he did.

A moment later, she stepped into a tree…

No, she stepped into the opening of a cave.

This was where she'd been leading him.

Derek stepped inside behind her. It was cold in here but dry. The space stretched back into a narrow tunnel. He didn't know how far it went, but, here at the mouth, it was wide enough to set up a temporary camp.

Staying here would be an answer to prayer. He'd do whatever was necessary to help his brother and get out of here.

He glanced behind him one more time. He didn't see the men.

Last time he checked, they were still scrambling down toward the river to try to rescue their friend. Hopefully, they wouldn't think to check here.

Autumn studied his face for a minute, almost as if she could read his mind. "That man probably won't make it. I hated to see that happen, but there was no way we could rescue him. It just wasn't safe."

"I understand." He looked around at the cave one more time. He needed to focus on their survival right now. "Do you think we'll be safe here? It seems like they might find us. Those men seemed pretty persistent."

"The cliff is still above us, and you can only see this cave if you're standing at the right angle since the opening right here is so narrow. Plus, a tree covers most of the mouth to this place. I feel like we'll be okay. But we need to keep our ears open, just in case."

"How did you even know this was here?"

She told him about the rescue that she'd done here about a year ago. As she did, Derek pictured it all playing out. He was sure Autumn had a lot of stories to tell from on the job. She seemed to love it.

"I can't even imagine what you see in the field," he said, lowering his backpack to the ground.

"You don't want to. It's the best and the worst of peo-

ple. Their worst nightmares and their greatest hopes…
sometimes." She put her bag on the floor also and let go
of Sherlock's leash. Her gaze seemed to access the space.

He didn't miss that *sometimes*. He hoped that he
wouldn't have to tack that on to the end of their story. He
hoped he would be able to find his brother and that everything would be okay, but he would be a fool not to prepare
himself for the worst-case scenario. The men after him
were ruthless, and if they had his brother…there was no
telling what they had done with him now.

He glanced around again at the dark space. "So what
now? What are you thinking?"

"We stay here until the danger passes. Those guys are
most likely going to help their friend. In the meantime, we
lie low and stay quiet."

"I can do that."

"When we're sure they're gone, we can grab some of
the dry wood from the shore. I've got a lighter, so we can
start a fire in here. This will give us some shelter when
the rain starts to come."

"Okay, let's do that."

Autumn paused, and her gaze locked with his. "After
the rain clears, we'll figure out our next step. I'm hoping
the towers come back up. I don't know if we're going to
get out of this without some backup."

Derek heard the concern in her voice, and a shudder
went down his spine. This was life or death, wasn't it?
It would only be by God's grace if they were able to get
out of it.

But he was thankful they had gotten this far.

Two hours later, the rain continued, just as torrential as
before. Autumn knew they were up high enough that they
should be safe from the floodwaters. But that still didn't

stop the flutters from invading her stomach. The situation had become precarious.

Derek found some wood that was dry enough that they were able to start a fire. The heat was welcome. However, she hoped that the smoke coming out of the cave didn't attract anybody.

Nobody in their right mind would be out in this weather right now. Even though those men knew the general direction in which she, Derek and Sherlock had come, there was no way they could get to them right now.

That was good news.

As she sat by the fire staring at the flames, she tried to focus on everything she had to be thankful for. Starting with the fact that Sherlock was okay.

She reached over and ran a hand down the length of her dog's back. He looked up at her with his blue eyes before leaning into her touch.

"The dog loves you," Derek said as he sat across from her, the fire separating them.

"He's been very faithful and very loyal to me. I can't complain about that."

"No, you can't."

Autumn knew she shouldn't bring this up, but she needed to keep her thoughts occupied. For that reason, she asked, "So you were engaged?"

Derek glanced down at his arms, which rested on the top of his knees, before looking back to Autumn. "I was. She actually left me at the altar."

Autumn's eyes widened. "Man, I can't imagine. I'm sorry to hear that. Did she ever give you an explanation?"

"She said that she felt like marrying me was what was expected of her, and she didn't want to live an expected life."

She watched his steady expression. She couldn't read

his feelings on the matter. Was he heartbroken? Or did he agree? "And how about you? How did you feel?"

He released a slow breath. "Initially? I was hurt. I'm a planner. I like to know where things are going. But after a while, I realized her words were true. We were great friends, and friendship is a great basis for marriage. But you also need some spark, some passion."

"I can understand that it was still difficult."

He frowned. "It was. People just expected us to get married. And it wasn't that I didn't love her, nor was it the fact that we couldn't have made it work. But we did feel more like friends than we did two people who were madly in love with each other."

"At least you came to that realization. That's important."

Derek nodded. "It was. My life today doesn't look anything like I thought it would. But that's just all a part of living, isn't it?"

"Yes, it is."

He shifted, pulling his gaze from the fire to Autumn. "What about you? How did you and your husband meet?"

"We were both rangers. We met when I started working here at this park. We couldn't stand each other at first, and then…one day we realized we actually loved each other."

"Sounds like a nice story."

"It was. Kevin was a good guy. The world lost someone good when he passed away."

"Have you dated since?" Derek visibly cringed as the words left his lips. "I'm sorry. I shouldn't ask these questions."

"No, it's okay. I know we're stuck out here with nothing but time on our hands right now." Truthfully, Autumn didn't really mind talking about it, even though she didn't do it very often. There was something about Derek that made him very easy to talk to. "No, I haven't dated very much since then. I haven't really felt the desire to, you know?"

He nodded, understanding in his gaze. "I know that all too well."

She felt such an immediate bond with this man that it scared her. She wasn't supposed to feel this way. She wasn't supposed to feel anything for anyone other than Kevin.

She glanced outside the cave and noticed that the rain was letting up.

A rumble of hunger sounded in her gut. She was starving. If they were going to be stuck out here much longer, they were going to need more supplies.

"Do you know what?" Autumn said, suddenly feeling restless. "I think I'm going to peek outside for a minute. I'll be right back."

He nodded and said nothing.

Autumn stepped out and discovered her theory was true. The rain was just a drizzle, at least, for a moment. She glanced around but didn't see any signs of the men. If they were smart, they were long gone by now.

Looking down, she saw something on one of the tree limbs below. Was that…a backpack?

It certainly looked like it.

She called back into the cave for Derek. "I need your help."

He stepped outside, and his eyes widened. "It's William's. The water must have carried it downstream."

"That would be a good thing for us. Did he have food inside?"

"He sure did."

"We're going to need to retrieve that."

What was William's backpack doing here? Derek had no idea about the answer to that question, but he saw this as an answer to prayer. The only thing he wasn't sure about was how they could safely retrieve it without being swept away in the floodwaters themselves.

"If you take my hand, I think I can reach it," Autumn said. "It's there at the rocky ledge, and the floodwater's just beneath it."

"Are you sure that's safe?" Concern ricocheted through him as he imagined how this would play out.

Autumn frowned, though the expression quickly disappeared as if she wanted to hide it. "I think I can do it. We need to try at least."

After a moment of hesitation, Derek nodded. This wasn't just something they were doing for fun. This was a matter of survival. If they were careful...

"I'm going to climb down the side, and when I get to that ledge below, that's when I'm going to need you to get on your belly and to hold on to my hand. I'll stretch out and see if I can reach it. Let's just pray this works."

"I've already started praying." Derek's words were true. He wouldn't stop praying until they were safe.

Autumn offered him a soft smile before beginning her descent down the rock wall. Derek held his breath as he watched, but he realized that the woman was capable. Still, in these conditions, nothing was certain.

Sherlock stood beside Derek, watching Autumn also. It was almost as if the dog was worried as well.

Once Autumn reached the ledge below, she looked up at Derek, her gaze intense and focused. "I'm ready now."

Just as he'd been instructed, he got on his belly and reached forward. He took her outstretched hand and held on tightly to it. Whatever he did, he could not let go.

With one more glance back at him, Autumn reached down.

Derek held his breath, praying their plan would work. She could almost reach the bag but not quite.

"Can you move forward any more and still be safe?" Autumn asked.

Derek scooted forward, his chest pressing into the rock beneath him. He still had enough leverage to hold him up here, but all this made him uncomfortable. It was too uncertain. He liked things to be black and white, right or wrong, up or down. Everything felt like it was in the balance right now.

"How's this?"

With obvious strain on her face, she reached down again. Her arm pulled in his grasp, and if his grip somehow slipped, he knew without a doubt that she'd go tumbling to her death.

He couldn't let that happen.

Autumn gave one more groan and gave it one last try. Her teeth seemed to grit as her lips pulled back with intense concentration.

Her fingers were mere inches away from that backpack. Maybe not even that much. If she could just reach a little farther…

Derek shifted just a little more, praying this wasn't a fatal error.

As he did, Autumn gave one last burst of effort. Her fingers enclosed the handle of the backpack.

She had it!

But it was too early for to feel victorious.

Derek helped pull her back upright until she was pressed against the ledge again. She handed the backpack up to him, the relief on her face obvious.

"Now if you could help me get back up here, I think I want to stay put for a while," she said.

Derek couldn't blame her. He climbed on his knees to give himself a little more arm room. Then he took her hand and helped her climb up the cliff.

As soon as she reached the ledge where Derek was, she collapsed. Sherlock licked her face, almost as if he understood what she was feeling.

Derek wanted nothing more than to hug her. How many of these situations were the two of them going to find themselves in? One after another, apparently.

"You okay?" Derek placed a hand on her back, feeling like she just needed human touch to let her know she wasn't in this alone.

She nodded and rolled to her side before lying on her back and staring at the sky. Her breaths came quickly, laced with exertion and adrenaline. "Yes, but I did see my life flash before my eyes back there."

Derek lowered himself to the ground, trying to catch his breath as well. "If there's anybody I had to be stuck out here with, I'm glad it's you."

She let her head fall to the side as she glanced at him and a grin stretched over her face. "I appreciate your vote of confidence."

"I mean it. You're…amazing."

"Thank you." She pushed herself up on her elbows before finally sitting up completely. She let out a long breath before saying, "You ready to see what's inside your brother's backpack?"

The brief amount of relief Derek had felt disappeared. It didn't really make any sense why a new grip of anxiety squeezed at him. But despite the illogical nature of the emotion, it was still there.

What if he found something incriminating inside his brother's backpack? He was about to find out. He prayed for grace and wisdom in the coming moments.

EIGHT

Autumn and Derek waited until they were back in the cave before they opened the backpack.

Autumn raised the bag toward Derek. "Would you like to do the honors?"

He shook his head, his gaze burdened with unseen pressures and questions. "You can go ahead. You know what you're looking for more than I do."

She nodded before unzipping the first compartment. She began pulling out some food. Granola bars. Peanuts. Beef jerky. Water.

"Almost all of it still looks good," she said.

That was a blessing, because they were going to need some more nourishment to sustain them, especially if this lasted much longer.

"We sealed everything in airtight bags to protect it against the elements and so that animals wouldn't be able to follow the scent of it."

That would prove very handy now. Autumn didn't know about Derek, but she was hungry.

She continued to dig into the depths of the bag and found a flashlight, a compass and even a blanket that had been rolled up. It was wet, but maybe they could dry it out. It would come in handy tonight.

Some clean clothing was inside, also packed in plastic bags. Derek could certainly wear some of it, and Autumn might even trade in her shirt for one of the sweatshirts in there. Warm, dry clothing sounded nice.

Really nice.

"Nothing out of the ordinary yet?" Derek said, his voice sounding thinner than usual.

Autumn glanced up at him. He seemed more nervous than she had expected him to be. Did he know something she didn't? Was he hiding something?

She didn't think so. She thought she could trust the man. But she had to be careful still. Too much was working against her right now.

Autumn supposed they were about to find out.

As she reached the bottom of the backpack, her hand hit fabric. There was nothing there.

"It's empty," she muttered.

Derek's shoulders slumped, as if he was relieved, and he ran a hand over his face.

"Why are you so nervous?" She studied his face.

"Nervous?" He shrugged before releasing a long breath, almost as if he had decided he should no longer be fake. "William and I have drifted apart in recent years. But he's always been more of the take-life-by-the-horns kind of guy. If he sees something he wants, he goes after it."

"And that's a bad thing?"

"I've always figured that those traits could go one of two ways. He would either be wildly successful or he'd find himself in a heap of trouble. Unfortunately, both of those qualities can masquerade as the other."

"Wise words." Had William gotten himself into some kind of trouble? She hadn't found anything to indicate that. Not yet, at least.

Autumn glanced back down at the backpack. It still felt too heavy, like she'd missed something.

"Let me just double-check a few more things to be certain," she said. "I can't help but feel there's something else in here."

She looked into all of the pockets and zippered compartments one more time to make sure she hadn't missed anything. It appeared she hadn't.

At the very bottom, she felt a zipper. Her pulse raced. What was this?

"What?" Derek leaned closer, a knot forming between his eyes.

She said nothing, simply tugged the zipper, listening as it buzzed around the bottom perimeter of the backpack.

A moment later, a hidden compartment was revealed. Two Ziploc bags rested at the bottom.

She glanced at Derek before carefully pulling the first one out. Whatever was inside, it was lightweight.

But it had been hidden for a reason.

Carefully, she opened it. She wished she had gloves in case this was some kind of evidence. But these were extraordinary circumstances, and right now she just had to concentrate on survival.

She laid the items out on the floor of the cave and studied them by the firelight. The first was a picture of William with a woman.

"That's his ex-girlfriend." Derek scooted closer to see.

Autumn could feel his body heat next to her. The realization caused an unexpected surge of electricity to rush through her, and she had to catch her breath for a minute.

Why was she having this reaction to the man?

She needed to stay focused.

Autumn picked up the photo and stared at a picture of the pretty blonde. "Nice-looking couple."

"That's Brooke. She looked nice, and she knew it."

Autumn pointed at the dark-haired man in the photo. "You and your brother look a lot alike."

Derek leaned closer. "We do. I've always been told that. But if you look at William, you'll see that he has a sparkle in his gaze. It's like he can't contain that little rakish part of himself that is amused by trouble."

Autumn looked up at Derek, more curious than ever. When she realized how close their faces were, she felt the breath leave her lungs.

She had to get a grip here.

She cleared her throat. "When did he and his girlfriend break up?"

He rubbed his jaw. "Probably four months ago. They'd been together for about a year."

"Who called it off?"

"As far as I know, he did. Said there was too much drama."

Autumn nodded and put the photo down, moving on to the next item. It was a string of numbers that had been handwritten on a torn piece of paper—maybe part of an envelope based on the thin line of dried adhesive on one side.

"Any idea what these numbers mean? It's too long to be a phone number." She counted the numbers one more time. "Too long to be a Social Security number as well."

"Could it be a routing number? Maybe to a checking account?"

Autumn looked more closely. "It's a possibility."

"I wish I could tell you that something was familiar. But I have no idea why William might have brought that information with him."

Autumn pulled out the second bag. It was smaller.

A cell phone. She hit the button and saw it still had some power.

"William didn't tell me he was bringing that," Derek muttered.

"Good to know we have that, at least."

Autumn checked the bottom of the backpack one more time, just to make sure she hadn't missed anything. As she did, her fingers brushed something at the very bottom.

She pulled out another bag, and her eyes widened when she saw the stack of money. She fanned the bills out and estimated that there had to at least be ten thousand dollars here.

"Any idea why your brother would be carrying this much money?" She studied Derek's face. Had she believed him too easily? Was there more to his story than he'd let on?

Derek's eyes looked as wide and surprised as Autumn felt. "I have no idea. It honestly makes no sense to me at all. I could understand if William brought a little cash, just in case he needed it. But carrying that kind of money with you? It's like he was just asking for trouble."

Autumn nodded. Her thoughts were the same.

What exactly was William hiding from his brother?

An hour later, Derek had changed into some of his brother's dry clothing. Autumn also donned a pair of his brother's sweatpants and a sweatshirt. The rest of their clothes dried near the fire, which they sat around right now.

They'd all dined on some of the food in William's backpack. Even Sherlock had enjoyed some beef jerky. The dog was just as hungry as the rest of them, and Derek was more than happy to share their stash of food with the canine. Sherlock had been a lifesaver, and they wouldn't be here without him.

But mostly what Derek was thinking about were those items William had brought with him. He could understand the picture of Brooke. Maybe William hadn't gotten over her.

Maybe all the suspicious contents had been left over from something else?

He might've believed that if it wasn't for the wad of cash in that compartment. A person didn't easily forget about ten thousand dollars in the bottom a backpack.

But Derek couldn't make sense of why William would bring that much money. Was his brother planning some kind of escape? To leave from here and start a new life? To pay somebody off when their trip was over? No matter which way Derek looked at it, it still didn't make any sense.

The unanswered questions caused a throb to begin in his head.

He closed his eyes and leaned toward the fire again. Despite everything that had happened, he had a lot to be thankful for. Starting with this fire. This cave. And Autumn, of course.

The woman stared into the flames right now, her face looking pensive as the flickers of orange warmed her features. But he knew her well enough to know her brain never seemed to turn off. Certainly she was trying to think through possible escape routes for this situation.

All of her law enforcement training couldn't have possibly prepared her for all of this.

Outside, the rain continued to fall. Occasionally, he checked the status of the river. It was still swollen, but it wasn't anywhere close to reaching the cave. That was another blessing.

Autumn had chosen wisely when she'd led them here.

With a sigh, Autumn reached down and grabbed the radio again. "I'll try one more time to see if I can reach anybody. It's worth a shot, right?"

"I'd say so."

She pressed the button and spoke into it. "This is Ranger Autumn Mercer. Is anyone out there?"

She waited as static filled the line.

Derek's stomach dropped. It was just like every other time they'd tried to make contact. Nothing.

But they couldn't give up hope. Eventually those towers would be operational again.

Just then, the radio crackled. Someone said something. Between the static, the words all ran together.

Excitement lit in Autumn's eyes. She jumped to her feet and paced toward the cave's opening. "This is Ranger Mercer—who is this?"

"This is Ranger Tom Hendrix. Are you doing okay, Ranger Mercer?"

"Ranger Hendrix." Relief filled her voice. "I can't tell you how good it is to hear your voice. We're stuck out here during the storm and need assistance. We have an injured man."

"We?"

She glanced at Derek. "I'm with a camper whose brother is injured and missing."

A camper? Something about the professional tone of her voice did something to his heart. He'd felt more like a friend than he wanted to admit.

The thought was ridiculous, though. They were just two people who'd been thrown together in extraordinary circumstances, and nothing more. The sooner he realized that, the better.

"There are also some gunmen out here. They've been following us. I have no doubt they're dangerous. They may even be holding someone captive right now."

"What are your coordinates?" Hendrix asked.

"We're just off the Meadow Brook River."

"I don't like to hear that. The roads have washed out.

We're still trying to clean up some downed trees as well. The earliest I can see us getting to you is tomorrow evening, and that's being optimistic."

Autumn's shoulders slumped. "What about a copter? Can you send one of those?"

"Not until the storms die down. It's quite the system going over us. It just seems to be lingering here. The rain will die down but, as you probably know, it's not very long before it starts up again. It's just not safe to be out in these high winds."

"That's what I thought. Are ATVs out of the question as well?"

"They are. We can't make it past the river."

"Okay." Autumn frowned and leaned down to pet Sherlock, who'd followed her.

"At least the towers are back up," he said. "I promise you, we're going to get to you as soon as we can. Is there anything else you need?"

"Just a lot of prayers," she said with a frown. She glanced back at Derek and shrugged, as if making sure he was listening.

"I understand. You've got those. The storm spawned a tornado about three miles west from you. Three people lost their homes. Numerous county roads are blocked. And people are in danger everywhere due to the flooding. It's a bad situation for all of us."

"Just get help here soon as you can, okay?" Autumn's voice filled with compassion.

"Will do. Over and out."

As Autumn lowered the radio, Derek knew she was fighting despair. He saw it in her gaze. In the way she nibbled her bottom lip.

She would probably never speak any of it aloud. And

he could appreciate that. But the emotion was still there, lingering in the depths of her eyes. This situation was dire.

She walked back toward him but didn't have to say anything. Her frown said it all.

"I'm sorry," Derek said. "I can't shake the feeling that this is all my fault."

"You and your brother couldn't have known when you set up camp that all of this would happen." She lowered herself across from him near the fire.

"No, I suppose we couldn't. But I still feel responsible." Derek was always the prepared one. How had things gone so wrong? Then again, how could someone prepare for all this?

Autumn offered another soft smile. "We'll get out of this. One way or another, we're going to get through it."

She was still thinking about other people, even in the middle of what had to feel like a crisis of her own. That had to be admired.

Just then, her radio crackled again.

Autumn and Derek exchanged glances before she lifted it to her mouth. "This is Ranger Autumn Mercer. Repeat."

"We are looking for you," a deep voice said.

Something about that voice didn't sound professional, not like another ranger getting back to her. No, the person on the other end almost sounded menacing.

"Who is this?" Autumn asked.

"We will find you," the man said. "And we are not going to give up until we do."

Autumn and Derek exchanged a look.

This was one of the gunmen pursuing them. He'd somehow managed to get hold of a radio and had heard Autumn's conversation with the ranger.

Derek's stomach sank at the realization.

These men knew that Autumn, Derek and Sherlock were stuck out here until tomorrow evening.

The good news was that Autumn hadn't given out their exact location.

Still, things had taken another grim turn.

He began praying for whatever tomorrow had in store.

NINE

Autumn didn't like any of this.

The news just seemed to be getting worse and worse by the moment. They were trapped out here with the men. Despite the treacherous situation, their leader had still found a way to taunt and threaten them.

The man was relentless.

She ran her hand across Sherlock's back, thankful for the dog's presence. Sherlock had always brought her so much comfort, even now. She stared into the fire for a minute, mesmerized by the flames and trying to sort her thoughts.

She picked up the photo of William and Brooke again and stared at it. "Is there any chance that somebody could have grabbed William thinking it was you?"

Derek's eyebrows shot up. "What do you mean?"

"Let's just say this wasn't random. Let's say somebody followed you guys out here. What if they saw William with you? Then they realized they grabbed the wrong person and that's why they're coming after us now."

A knot formed between his eyebrows, and he shook his head. "I'm not sure why anybody would come after me."

"You're an attorney, right?" Her voice perked. Maybe she was on to something.

"That's right." He nodded slowly, uncertainly, like he didn't like where this conversation was going.

"You've certainly made a lot of people mad, at least if you're anything like many attorneys. Lawyers make enemies. Am I right?"

He nodded. "I can't deny that. But I haven't had any explicit threats lately, if that's what you're saying."

She leaned closer. "Let's not think lately. Let's just think at all. Has anyone ever threatened your life?"

"Plenty of people, though I think most of those were just empty threats." Derek let out a breath. "I know that's not helpful, so let me think a little deeper here."

He paused, staring into the fire, and Autumn gave him time to think. Certainly, he had a lot of cases to think through. She didn't want to rush him.

"There was one man I put in prison after a drunk driving episode," he finally said. "He got out last year, though, and I haven't heard anything from him. There was another sailor I had put in prison for murder, but he's in there for life. I can't imagine him coming after me now."

"Anyone else?" Autumn stared at him, hoping they'd find some answers through this conversation.

Derek's eyes widened, as if he'd remembered something. "There was this one guy. He went to jail after beating his wife. I know he was up for parole. But he was definitely angry at me. Said that I had made up evidence and things like that. Of course, I didn't. But this guy was in denial. He honestly couldn't see where he had done anything wrong, even though his wife had plenty of bruises to prove it."

Autumn swallowed hard. Was this the information they'd been looking for? If they could figure out who the guys were and why they were pursing them, maybe they could outwit them at this game.

"What was his name?" Autumn asked.

"Owen Perkins."

"You don't know for sure if he got out on parole, though? Right?"

"I've been out here for the past four days, and my brother and I both made a promise not to bring cell phones." Derek glanced at the device that had been found in his brother's backpack. "Obviously, my brother didn't feel as serious about that as I did."

"I guess he didn't."

"What are the chances that we have service out here?" Derek stared at her.

Autumn shrugged. "Honestly, there's no telling. Service is iffy on a good day. But with the storms we've been having…it's anyone's guess."

He grabbed the phone and hit the button. "I need to figure out what my brother's passcode is."

"You have some good guesses?"

"How hard could it be? I'll try his birthday first." He typed something in and frowned.

It obviously hadn't worked.

"Maybe my parents' anniversary…" he muttered.

Autumn scooted closer. "Any success?"

"No, and one more try and I'll be locked out." He paused and pressed his lips together. "There's only one other possibility I can think of. Let's hope this works. It's the birthday of our childhood dog, Muffins. William always loved that dog."

Autumn's breath caught when she saw the screen on the phone flicker on.

It had worked.

Her gaze went to the battery level. It only had ten percent left. They needed to use that ten percent carefully. There was only one bar—but at least there *was* a bar.

"Should I search for information about Owen Perkins

or should we try to call somebody?" Derek stared at her, waiting for her before proceeding.

"Since I've already talked to Ranger Hendrix, I don't think there's anybody else who can do anything for us. Go ahead and search."

He typed in that man's name, and they waited. The phone was slow to load the search results.

But finally, the page filled.

Derek sucked in a quick breath.

"What is it?" Autumn asked.

He turned toward her, his eyes wide. "Owen was released from jail two days ago."

"You really think he is the one who might be out there coming after us?" Autumn asked.

"I think it's a really good place to start at least."

All Derek could think about was the fact that Owen Perkins had been released from jail.

Owen had always given Derek a bad feeling. Something about the man was off and dangerous.

Was it really possible that the man might be coming after him now? He didn't want to believe it. Yet, at the same time, he wanted some type of logic in this situation. Nothing made sense right now.

He sat by the entrance of the cave. It was his turn to keep watch. Sherlock stayed beside him, even though the dog's eyes occasionally closed. Derek was certain that if the canine heard anything, he would be instantly alert.

All Derek saw right now was darkness and the occasional drips of rain coming from the entrance of the cave. The rushing of the river actually sounded rather soothing. If circumstances were different, maybe he would actually sleep well right now.

But too much was at stake. Too much was on his mind.

He glanced back at Autumn. She'd used the blanket that his brother had been carrying with him. She wrapped it over her and used the backpack as a pillow as she laid near the fire.

He was supposed to wake her up at two thirty so they could trade duty. But he doubted he would. She needed her rest, especially if all this turned out to be his fault.

The two of them had talked before Autumn laid down. They decided first thing in the morning, they would try to track the gunmen again. It was the only way they could think of to locate William.

Once they found wherever these guys were staying, they couldn't make a move. They would need to wait for backup. But maybe, in the meantime, they could get their eyes on William and figure out if he was okay or not.

Derek lifted another prayer. He really hoped that his brother was okay. Every time he closed his eyes, images of William being hurt or in pain filled his mind. He couldn't handle it.

William had never been a great little brother. He mostly thought of himself. But that didn't mean he deserved anything bad to happen to him. Derek had always gone to bat for his brother, and he would do it again now.

But he still couldn't understand why William had brought so much money with him.

Derek thought about that number sequence again. What could that possibly mean?

He had to believe that his brother had packed those things on purpose. The money. The photo. The cell phone. Even the name with the numbers below it.

His brother had obviously known something that he hadn't bothered to share with Derek.

A bad feeling turned inside Derek at the thought. Secrets were rarely a good thing. He'd prosecuted enough cases to know that. But would his brother purposefully put them in danger? He didn't want to think that could be true.

Just then, Sherlock's ears perked. He stood on all fours, a low growl escaping from his depths.

Derek straightened and stared outside, trying to prepare for the worst.

He saw nothing.

But the dog had obviously heard something.

He grabbed his flashlight and shined it outside, trying to find a source of whatever it was that bothered Sherlock.

It was so dark. It was hard to see anything, even with his flashlight.

But only one thought remained in his head.

What if those men had found them again?

Autumn jerked from her sleep.

What was that sound?

Suddenly, she forgot all about resting and warmth and getting sleep.

Sherlock was letting them know that something was wrong.

She scrambled to her feet and grabbed her gun. She hurried toward the entrance of the cave and crouched beside Derek as he shined his flashlight outside.

"Do you see anything?" she asked, one hand reaching for her gun.

"No, nothing. Just darkness, the cliff face and rain. Maybe Sherlock only thought he heard something."

She wished for sanity's sake that she could believe that. "No, not Sherlock. His instincts are great. He's never let me down. Can I see the flashlight?"

Derek handed it to her. She shined it outside as well but, just like Derek said, she also saw nothing.

Tension snaked up her spine. What could have triggered Sherlock? Had those men found them again?

She also knew there were other dangers out here in the nighttime, especially in these conditions. The three of them weren't the only ones who were looking for shelter right now.

So were the wild animals who called this place home. The beam of the flashlight illuminated everything around her one more time. She stopped as something reflected back to her.

Two things, actually.

Two eyes.

Probably about six feet from the cave.

Her breath caught.

"What is that?" Derek whispered.

"If I had to guess?" Her throat went dry. "A bobcat."

Derek stared at her a minute, as if making sure he'd heard correctly. "This isn't good."

"No, it's not." She put her hand on top of Sherlock's back, trying to soothe the animal. "It's okay, boy. Heel."

The last thing she wanted was for her dog to get into a fight with a wildcat. She wanted to keep Sherlock safe just as much as the dog wanted to protect her.

"Derek, go grab one of the sticks from the fire. Try to get one that's burning on the end, if you can. That will scare our visitor off for now."

He didn't argue or ask questions. Instead, he rushed over to do exactly as she had told him.

He returned a moment later with a makeshift torch. Autumn took it from him and held it out at the entrance of the cave. As she did, the light illuminated the bobcat. The creature had come closer. He was probably only two feet away now.

Tension filled her as the implications of the situation flooded her mind. This could be deadly.

She prayed it didn't come to that.

Sherlock let out another low growl. He could sense the danger, too, couldn't he?

Autumn just hoped this worked. She had her gun, but she didn't want to use it on the animal.

There had been a wildcat attack two weeks ago. These creatures weren't above doing that, even though they were usually fairly docile unless threatened or sick.

"I don't think the fire is scaring him," Derek whispered.

"Just give it a minute." Autumn hoped her words were true. Normally, experts said to spray cats with water. She didn't have a spray bottle with her, however.

She'd never actually come face-to-face with one of these creatures. She'd seen plenty of them from a distance. But they usually ran away as soon as they saw a human.

This cat might be desperate, though. Hurt? It was a possibility. But she thought it was more likely that the storm had confused the animal. Maybe floodwaters had wiped out its home. She didn't know. She just knew this cat could not come in this cave right now. It would be a fight for the territory, if it did.

"I think it's still coming closer," Derek whispered.

Autumn agreed. That didn't make sense. The cat should be running away from the fire.

Unless the cat was desperate. Desperate usually meant aggressive.

Dear Lord, please protect us now. I know I keep asking that, but I just can't seem to stop. The danger keeps coming.

"Do me a favor," Autumn said. "Go get one more stick. Maybe this one's not bright enough."

Derek rushed away to do as she asked.

When he got back, she held both of the sticks outside

the cave and shoved them toward the cat, trying to scare
the beast away.

But the glowing eyes just stared back at her.

She had no idea if this was going to work.

TEN

Derek didn't like this. It was one thing to pit man against man. But pitting man against nature was an entirely different story. And both of those things at once?

It was nothing but trouble.

This whole camping trip had just been a bad idea.

"Let me hold one of the sticks for you," Derek said.

Autumn gave him one, and he extended his arm outside the cave. He held the fire toward the cat, praying that it would scare the feline off.

The cat stood defiant.

In fact, it appeared that the creature was slowly creeping forward. An animal that brave…it was unnerving.

"Do you think it wants our food?" Derek asked.

"It's a possibility. As a matter fact, why don't you go get a piece of that jerky right now?"

Derek had sealed everything back up, but he knew animals had great senses of smell. The beast could be hungry for food and could have sensed it.

Quickly, he unwrapped one of the sticks and brought it back to Autumn. "What are you going to do now?"

"I'm going to throw it away from the cave."

"Won't the cat fall into the river?"

"Bobcats are great climbers. He should able to go down there and retrieve it. He'll be okay."

Derek was going to have to trust her on that. It beat the alternatives—being attacked or having to use one of their last bullets.

As the cat continued to creep closer, Autumn held out the food. The cat paused.

Derek crouched back, half expecting the cat to attack.

The next instant, Autumn tossed the food onto the riverbank below.

He held his breath, waiting to see what would happen.

The cat leaped away from them.

Autumn's plan had worked. But how long would they be safe? Would the bobcat return?

Derek released a pent-up breath. "Can we stay here?"

"I'm hoping that's going to hold that cat off for a while. But we're definitely going to need to stay here just in case. It's not safe for us to travel. It's too dark. Too wet. We have to choose our poison. Face the cat? Or face sliding off into the river?"

It wasn't a choice that he wanted to make.

"If we stay here, we remain on guard," Autumn said. "Unless you need to get some sleep. If that's the case, fine. I can take over duty."

"I'll be fine."

No way was Derek going to let her face this alone. Not if he could help it.

But that situation had been too close for his comfort.

As they sat at the entrance of the cave, Autumn glanced at Derek.

The man had surprised her.

Most guys liked to be in charge. But he seemed comfortable enough with his own masculinity to let her call the shots. She appreciated that quality about him.

Yet, at the same time, he didn't seem weak. His humility only made him seem more secure. If Autumn had to battle his ego as well as the elements and the gunmen…it would be an entirely different story right now.

She counted her blessings.

She tried to put herself in his shoes. The man had been left at the altar. It couldn't have been easy.

Derek was accomplished. He was handsome. And he was obviously smart.

In some ways, he reminded her of her husband. It was the strangest thing, because, when she looked at Derek, she felt a flutter of nerves sweep through her.

She hadn't felt those things in a long time, nor had she thought she ever would feel those emotions again.

But something about Derek was different. They made a good team. Autumn couldn't say that about very many people.

Just then, Sherlock stood from her side, walked over to Derek and lay down beside him.

Traitor.

Yet she couldn't fault the dog. Seeing that Sherlock trusted Derek only reaffirmed that she could trust him as well. The sight warmed her heart.

At once, a memory filled her. An image of her and her husband sitting in the screened-in porch behind their house. One of their favorite things to do was to sit back there during rainstorms, listening to the drops hitting the tin roof.

She smiled.

Those were the moments she missed the most. The simple times.

Now she sat out there with Sherlock and listened. Something about the sound soothed her. But, if she was honest with herself, it also left her feeling lonely.

"You're looking at me." Derek studied her in curiosity.

Autumn looked away and let out a little laugh. "I guess I was. I'm sorry."

"What are you thinking?"

She swallowed hard, contemplating what to say. "Just that you surprised me."

He raised an eyebrow. "Surprised you how?"

"You seem like a good man, Derek." It was honest but safe and not too revealing.

He offered up a smile. "I'd like to think so. I try, at least."

"Are you ready to return to DC?" She could wonder about his life outside all of this. What did he do when he wasn't working? Did he have a full social life? Was he happy?

"Funny that you ask that." He shifted, rubbing Sherlock's head. "I'm actually at the point in my career where I need to figure out what I want to do next. I thought it was private practice. But the firm I joined keeps me even busier than I'd been at JAG. Sometimes I'd like a slower pace of life."

"What are you leaning toward?"

He shrugged, his gaze scanning the area around the cave. "I'm not sure. There are days when I think that this is the career I want to stay in forever. And there are other times when I would like to get outside DC."

"I can understand that. It wasn't easy for me to leave my old career behind. But it was the best choice I ever made. I never would have met Kevin if I didn't."

"You really love being out here, don't you?"

She shrugged. "When I'm outside, I can usually figure

things out a little bit more. Life has a bit more clarity away from the busyness and technology."

"Even now?"

"Even now, believe it or not. There are lessons that we can learn in all kinds of situations in life. Including this one." She leaned forward and rubbed her hand against Sherlock's back, trying not to feel jealous that Sherlock had chosen Derek.

"I agree with you. Very wise words. Seems like you might need a vacation when all this is done."

She let out a little laugh before sobering. "You know, I actually haven't had a vacation in years."

"Not since your husband died?"

"I didn't even take one after he died. I couldn't. The thought of sitting at our house all by myself… I couldn't handle it. So I threw myself into my work."

"And how did that work for you?"

"Maybe the jury is still out on that one. I'm not sure. Some days I feel like I've grown by leaps and bounds, and other days I feel like I'm right back to where I started."

"That sounds like the nature of grief."

The two of them shared a moment of silence, and she felt something pass between them. Did Derek?

She leaned her head against a rock opening, feeling exhaustion washing over her.

She wasn't sure if Derek felt anything or not. But she had other things to think about right now. Things other than romance and romantic feelings. Or if she could possibly fall in love again one day.

But at least she felt some hope.

There was a lot to be said for that.

As soon as the sun rose and the rain let up the next morning, Derek, Autumn and Sherlock departed. They left the majority of their things in the cave and planned on coming back tonight if necessary. Truth was, Derek hoped they were rescued before then. But, if they weren't, at least they had a home base.

As he remembered the events from last night, Derek wasn't sure how much longer that would be the case. Especially if that bobcat came back again. They were intruding into its territory. Was there anywhere that was safe out here?

He wasn't sure.

Just as they had yesterday, Autumn led the way as they climbed the ledge above the river. *Don't look down*, he reminded himself.

Heights didn't bother him, but the sheer drop was enough to unnerve the most brazen person. The rapids almost seemed to taunt them. He was nearly certain the river had swollen even more after last night.

Sherlock looked like he had done this a million times as he followed behind Autumn. She still held on to his leash, just in case.

The good news was they hadn't run into those gunmen again.

Not yet.

Hopefully not again, though he knew that was wishful thinking.

Near the area where the one man had slipped yesterday, Autumn paused. She reached into a bush on the side of the cliff and grabbed something.

She held up a swatch of fabric. "I think this is a piece of the gunman's shirt. The branch must have caught it on its way down. This will help Sherlock lead us to this man."

"We can use whatever help we can get," Derek said. For a moment, he almost felt like that fabric was like the dove bringing back a twig to the ark. It offered them some semblance of hope.

Finally, the three of them reached the end of the ledge and climbed back onto solid ground. Autumn glanced around before motioning for Derek to follow. That must have meant that the coast was clear.

Still, they remain quiet as they moved through the woods. If those guys were out there, they didn't want to alert them that they were coming.

So far, it was working.

Autumn let Sherlock smell the fabric swatch. After sniffing, the dog began to pull her. A few minutes later, they stopped at the campsite where he and his brother had stayed.

There was hardly anything left. The tent was gone. Water covered the area where the fire pit had been.

"We have to keep moving," Autumn said.

He nodded and continued to follow, trying not to think about the implications of everything that had happened. He was thankful to be alive right now. If he hadn't found Autumn when he did, this might be an entirely different story.

He would probably be dead.

Autumn let Sherlock lead them through the dense, slick forest. They probably walked for twenty minutes, in the opposite direction of his old campsite.

As a new sound filled the air, Autumn turned around and pressed her finger to her lips, motioning for him to be quiet.

Derek knew what that meant. That they were close.

He joined her as she hid behind a tree. As they peered off into the distance, he saw that three tents had been set up.

He drew in a sharp breath when he spotted one of the

gunmen who'd been chasing them yesterday. The man sat outside by a campfire, poking it with a stick.

They had found them.

He, Autumn and Sherlock had found a gunman.

Now they needed to figure out what to do from here.

ELEVEN

"Now that we know where the gunmen are staying, we'll be able to lead the authorities back here," Autumn whispered. "We just need to be patient now."

"But my brother…" His voice faded wistfully.

"If we're all dead, we're not going to be able to help him." She knew this had to be hard on him, but they had to be careful.

"Can we stay couple more minutes? I'd just like to see if there's any signs of life." Derek's voice cracked with grief.

Autumn's heart pounded in her ears. She understood his dilemma. Though she didn't want to do anything to put the three of them in danger, she knew this was important to him.

"We'll stay a few more minutes," Autumn said. "Just promise me you're not going to try anything rash."

"I won't. I promise."

She believed him. He'd done nothing to show he couldn't be trusted.

The three of them remained perched in their hiding spot behind the trees. Autumn watched the campsite and saw the one man by the fire. She could only assume that another man had been swept away by the rapids. Still, the third man should have been shot in the shoulder during their first confrontation. That would just leave one more man.

The fight was becoming more evenly matched as time went on. But that still didn't mean that they would be able to take these men. Autumn had no idea how many weapons they had or how much ammunition.

Plus, these men were brutal. They didn't think anything about destroying human lives. That was evident in their actions.

Autumn, on the other hand, couldn't stop thinking about that man who had been swept downstream yesterday. Part of her wondered if she should've done more to help him.

Yet, she knew if she had, they'd all be dead right now. It didn't stop the ache in her heart. As a search and rescue ranger, her desire was to help people, not to destroy lives.

She continued to watch the campsite. The tents these men had…they were nice. Expensive.

Kind of like the camo clothing they wore.

Who were they? If these men really did have as much money as she assumed, that might rule out Owen Perkins. From what she understood from Derek, Owen didn't have that kind of money.

What about that money William was carrying with him? She struggled to put all the pieces together.

A few minutes later, another man left his tent and joined the first man by the fire. He had a sling around his arm.

This must be the man she'd shot.

The two of them muttered things to themselves, things that Autumn couldn't make out. But she had no doubt that they were most likely planning their next move.

Her stomach tightened at thought. She just knew they weren't done yet.

She wasn't sure how long Derek wanted to stay here.

They could afford to linger for a little bit longer, as long as they were careful. But being this close was risky.

The wind swept over the area again. If Autumn understood correctly, this would be the last of the system, and the storm should pass over them after this. She could only hope, at least.

The weather had been overwhelming. Without it, they would probably be back to safety right now. Maybe even with William. It was hard to know for sure.

Across the way, a squirrel scampered.

Autumn froze, placing her hand on Sherlock's head and praying the dog remained on duty. Squirrels were his weakness.

Plus, the critter had caught the gunmen's attention.

She watched as the men froze. They glanced around, looking for the source of the movement.

One of men reached for his gun.

They were ready for action, Autumn realized.

She glanced back at Derek. His face looked tense also.

They waited to see what would happen.

Dear Lord, keep us invisible. Please.

She'd never muttered so many desperate prayers before.

Finally, the men finally seemed to notice it was just a squirrel. They turned back to the fire and their conversation.

Autumn felt her lungs deflate.

That had felt close. Too close.

How much longer would they have to wait? She wanted to gather as much information as she could. But not to the point of putting them at risk.

Thirty minutes later, a third man emerged from the tent.

It was about time.

Autumn's breath caught.

The man hauled someone out behind him.

Derek's brother.

William.

He was alive.

Relief washed through her.

She glanced at Derek and saw his gaze fastened to the scene.

Thank goodness his brother was still alive.

But when Autumn saw the way William dragged his leg behind him, her hope turned into concern. Someone had used a stick and wrapped some cloth around the man's leg.

But he was still obviously in a lot of pain.

His face scrunched, and he let out a moan.

Derek caught his breath beside her, and she placed a hand on his arm. Her touch was partly in comfort and partly in warning. She feared he would act instinctually.

That could get them killed.

He continued to watch. One of the men tossed something to William. It appeared to be a package of food. Maybe an MRE—Meals Ready to Eat.

At least they were keeping William alive.

But even from where Autumn stood, she could see that Derek's brother was in bad shape. His lip appeared to be busted, his eye swollen and his clothes dirty. He had been through a lot.

How much longer would he survive out in these elements?

Autumn had no idea. But she didn't like this.

Derek felt the anger rising inside him. Why were these men holding his brother hostage? He obviously needed medical help. Seeing his strong and confident brother in this condition made Derek feel sick to his stomach. He wanted nothing more than to rush down there and rescue him.

But he knew that would be a bad idea. It would put them all in jeopardy.

Autumn glanced at him. She didn't have to say a word for Derek to know her thoughts.

It was time for them to leave.

They'd already been here too long. One wrong move and...

Autumn looked at him and nodded.

They turned away, cautiously maneuvering through the woods and careful not to say a word.

As they did, the rain started again. Sometimes it felt like it wasn't ever going to let up. At least they had somewhere dry to return to. At least, for now.

They waited until they were a good half a mile from the camp before Autumn turned to him and spoke.

"Now that you had a better look at these guys, did you recognize any of them?" she asked.

Derek had already thought about it and shook his head. "No, unfortunately, I didn't."

"So none of those guys were Owen Perkins?"

"They weren't. Nor did any of them look like anybody I ever saw with him. I'm not sure that he's our guy."

She frowned. "You're sure?"

He nodded. "I'm sure. I mean, Owen could be violent. He might even want to track me down. But I don't see him grabbing some friends and trekking through the wilderness to do that. He's a coward. He is more likely the type who would do a drive-by shooting or try to catch me by surprise."

"If that's the case, then we need to keep thinking. The more we can figure out about these guys, the better our chances of defeating them."

"I agree. I can't stop thinking about it. I just keep hoping that something will make sense. But it hasn't yet."

"And I still think we should consider that maybe it was something that William has gotten himself into."

"If that was the case, why do they keep chasing after us?"

"Maybe they think if they have us that will give them leverage over William."

His stomach clenched again. He didn't like the thought of that. Not one bit.

A hard wave of rain hit them, coming down steady and strong and making it hard to see anything in front of them.

"Stay close," Autumn said. "Unfortunately, this rain started just as we've reached the hardest part of the trail."

He nodded. What part of this process hadn't been hard? It seemed like every time they turned around, they hit a new obstacle.

He supposed he could relate this back to law school. He'd put in long, grueling hours. There were times he'd wanted to quit. But he hadn't. He'd pushed through until he reached his goal.

That's what they needed to do right now.

As they started to cross through the gorge area, Derek held his breath. This would definitely be the trickiest part of the walk back. But there was no way to get to the cave other than this route.

He watched best he could through his blurry eyes as Autumn carefully picked her steps in the rocky area.

Just as she reached the middle of the gorge, he heard a sound above them.

Was that thunder?

Something in his gut told him it wasn't.

He looked up just in time to see a mass of boulders tumbling toward them.

* * *

Autumn heard the rumbling and knew exactly what was happening.

She let go of Sherlock's leash and patted his back, signaling for him to run.

She tried to duck out of the way, but it was too late.

The ground disappeared from beneath her, and she began to tumble down the mountain.

As she looked down below, she knew how this could end.

First there was a cliff, and then a river.

Both were likely to kill her.

Swallowing a scream, she reached for something to grab. A rock. A branch. A tree.

But there was nothing but dirt and moving rocks.

The muddy ground around her continued to pull her down, leaving her feeling helpless.

She glanced in the distance one more time. She was only feet from the cliff.

She closed her eyes and lifted a prayer.

As she did, her hand swung forward and she grabbed a…branch?

She wrapped her fingers around it, and her body jerked to a halt. But not before momentum pulled her legs over the ledge.

She was literally hanging on by a thread right now.

Her head spun at the thought of it.

What about Derek? Had he gotten caught up in this, too?

She glanced up a time to see him run down the mountain toward her. Relief filled her. At least he was okay.

But what about Sherlock?

Her gaze traveled to the other side of the mudslide.

Sherlock carefully navigated the rocks as he rushed toward her.

The dog was fine.

Gratitude washed through her.

But she knew she wasn't out of trouble yet.

Especially when she heard the stick crack.

Her lifeline going to break any minute now.

"You've got to help me," she yelled.

Derek reached the ledge and bent toward her, his eyes assessing the situation. "We're going to get you. Just hang on."

"This branch isn't going to hold me. It's going to break any time now."

He nodded, his gaze serious and intense. "We've got you, Autumn."

Something about the way he said the words made her believe it.

He pulled the flannel shirt from his arms. While still holding on to one arm, he tossed the other end down to her.

"Can you grab hold of this?" he yelled. "We can use it as a rope. I can pull you up."

She stared at the sleeve, her throat feeling dry and achy.

Grabbing ahold of one lifeline would require letting go of the other.

Could she do this?

She had no other choice if she wanted to survive.

TWELVE

Derek's heart pounded in his ears as he realized what was at stake here.

Autumn's life.

He couldn't let her down now. He'd never forgive himself if he did.

"Is your footing stable?" Autumn yelled, her voice strained. "The whole ground is mush right now. I don't want to take you down with me."

Derek kicked his feet against the ground. The rocks beneath him seemed stable.

But he knew Autumn's words were true. One slipup and they'd both be goners.

He looked down at her and nodded. "I can handle this."

There was no time to waste. That branch was going to break any second now.

She stared at that flannel shirt for another moment. Derek knew it couldn't be easy to let go of that branch, that lifeline. It was the only thing keeping her alive. But this was the only way he could rescue her right now.

She drew in a deep breath, as if prepping herself to take action. The strain on her face grew deeper and her arms seemed to go slack, as if her muscles were weakening.

Finally, one of her hands left the stick. Her whole face

FREE BOOKS GIVEAWAY

2 FREE ROMANCE BOOKS!

2 FREE SUSPENSE BOOKS!

GET UP TO FOUR FREE BOOKS & TWO FREE GIFTS WORTH OVER $20!

We pay for everything!

**YOU pick your books –
WE pay for everything.**
You get up to FOUR New Books an
TWO Mystery Gifts...absolutely FRE

Dear Reader,

I am writing to announce the launch of a huge **FREE BOO**
GIVEAWAY... and to let you know that YOU are entitled to
choose up to FOUR fantastic books that WE pay for.

Try **Love Inspired® Romance Larger-Print** books and fall
in love with inspirational romances that take you on an
uplifting journey of faith, forgiveness and hope.

Try **Love Inspired® Suspense Larger-Print** books where
courage and optimism unite in stories of faith and love in
the face of danger.

Or TRY BOTH!

In return, we ask just one favor: Would you please
participate in our brief Reader Survey? We'd love to hear
from you.

This FREE BOOKS GIVEAWAY means that we pay for
everything! We'll even cover the shipping, and no purcha
is necessary, now or later. So please return your survey
today. You'll get **Two Free Books** and **Two Mystery Gifts**
from each series to try, altogether worth over **$20!**

Sincerely

Pam Powers

Pam Powers
For Harlequin Reader Servic

Complete the Survey below and return
it today to receive up to 4 FREE BOOKS
and FREE GIFTS guaranteed!

was tight with intensity under the pressure of what she had to do. But, as she reached forward, her hand wrapped around the flannel.

Good. This was a good start.

"Hold on to it with both hands," he said. "You can do it."

Derek braced his feet again, ready to hold her up. He hoped this worked, because he didn't have any other plan right now.

Autumn released her other hand and grabbed the shirt. Derek felt himself lurch forward. He caught in his balance and grunted as he shifted his balance.

Autumn didn't weigh much, but momentum pulled them forward, pulled them toward their death.

Derek saw the fear in her eyes, and he needed to reassure her. "I've got this."

As if Sherlock realized that they needed help, the dog jumped over the mudslide area in one bound. His teeth gripped the flannel shirt, and he helped Derek pull Autumn toward stable ground.

Two heaves later, Autumn was propelled back up on the cliff. On solid ground, she sprawled on top of the rocks beside him.

Derek leaned back and caught his breath as his heart raced in his chest.

That had been close. Too close.

He turned toward Autumn, placing a hand on her back. "Are you okay?"

She looked up, her limbs trembling and her eyes full of relief. "I am now. Thank you."

She turned over and rubbed Sherlock's head. The dog barked, almost as if he understood what had almost happened.

The two of them were quite the sight. They were a team. No one could deny that.

Derek had felt a part of their team the past couple days, and it had been a good feeling.

One he didn't want to end.

Derek wanted nothing more right now than to take Autumn into his arms. It was ridiculous, really. And he knew that.

But, in that moment when Autumn had been dangling over the cliff, he'd realized how quickly she'd gained a place in his heart. She'd been his rock while they were out here, and Derek knew that he would never be the same after this experience.

Autumn pushed herself up on her palms and released one more breath. "We're going to have to think of an alternate way to get back to that cave."

Derek looked up at the mudslide that consumed this section of the mountain. Yes, they would need an alternate plan if they wanted to get back to the cave.

But just how they were going to do that was an entirely different story.

Autumn felt weariness washing over her. That mudslide had taken more out of her than she wanted to let on. Her shoulder ached, there was a gash on her leg, and she was fairly certain her hip was bruised.

Still, she was grateful to be alive.

Thank goodness Derek and Sherlock had been there. If they hadn't been… She pushed away those thoughts. That had been too close.

Her life had flashed before her eyes—again.

She glanced up at the landscape around her and felt exhaustion pressing in. Going on two nights without hardly any rest was finally catching up with her. She only prayed that the backup rangers would be able to arrive today.

But as much as she wanted to believe that would happen, she was also doubtful. Until this rain let up, they were most likely going to be stuck out in these woods with those trigger-happy gunmen.

The three of them had to climb up the mountain and go over the ridge in order to skirt around the mudslide and get back to the cave. She kept telling herself she could do it, but her body wanted to shut down.

Her shoulder ached. A sharp pain went through her knee. Her head pounded.

She felt Derek's gaze on her, studying her, and she tried to pull herself together.

"Listen, maybe we should take a rest," Derek said.

She'd never been a good actor. Certainly, he could see the pain and discomfort written on her face. It was hard to hide.

Even though she didn't want to, she nodded. Maybe a little rest would be a good idea.

They found a boulder that was the perfect height for them to sit down and take a breather. She took her backpack off, grabbed a bottle of water and took a long sip. She then poured some for Sherlock.

Thankfully, the rain had stopped for now, but the wind coming behind it was chilly. It would have been bearable if not for their wet clothes and shoes.

"I should check out your leg," Derek said, pointing to the spot. "There's a cut near your knee."

She pulled up the leg of her pants and flinched when she saw the gash there.

"We should clean that," he said.

She nodded, trying to hold back her pain. "There's a first aid kit in my bag."

He riffled through the backpack until he found it. Then he poured some water on the wound, patted it dry and put some ointment on it. As the final step, he put a bandage over it.

Autumn felt her cheeks flush when she realized his care and concern.

Derek was a good guy, someone she would like to get to know more once this was all over.

If this ever ended. Sometimes it felt like that wouldn't happen.

"All better," he announced.

She looked away before he saw the growing affection in her gaze. "Thank you."

"So, what are you thinking?" Derek asked, staring off into the distance.

"I'm thinking that when this is all done, I want to take a long bath, read a good book and eat some Chinese food."

He chuckled. "That Chinese food does sound pretty nice right now."

She glanced at him, noticing just how handsome this man still looked, despite their circumstances. She wanted to know more about him, about what he was like outside of these circumstances.

"How about you?" she asked. "Besides reuniting with your brother, what are you most looking forward to?"

He rubbed his head. "You know what? I don't really know. Food sounds nice. Warm clothes sound nice. The only thing about the situation that's been good is—"

"Is what?" Autumn's heart pounded in her ears as she waited for him to finish.

Derek glanced at her. "You."

A surprising wave of delight rushed through her. She'd been hoping he would say that. Because she felt the same way.

The thought of Derek returning to DC, to his condo or

house or whatever it was, resuming life as if they had never met…the thought caused sadness to press on her.

So did the thought of her returning to her regular life. Back in her cozy but lonely cabin. Searching for ways to move on after Kevin had passed.

She'd never thought that she was ready to move on, but meeting Derek had changed that.

She realized that Derek was waiting for her response. "I'm really glad we were able to meet also. I just wish the circumstances had been different."

He let out a weary chuckle. "Me too."

"You know, we're pretty high up," she said. "Maybe I'll check one more time to see if we have radio reception."

"Sounds like a plan." Derek took a long sip of his water before pouring some into a bowl for Sherlock.

She pressed the button on her radio. "This is Ranger Autumn Mercer. Is anybody out there?"

She remembered yesterday when the gunman's voice had come over the line. She held her breath, praying that she wouldn't hear that same voice again.

Instead, Hendrix's voice came on the line. "Ranger Mercer, it's Hendrix."

Relief washed through her. "Any updates on the situation?"

"I'm afraid our hands are full right now. The roads are washed out, and we're doing everything we can to get the trees cleared. We tried to send a crew in by foot, but the river keeps stopping us. It's just a bad situation wherever we look."

She pressed her eyes closed. "So you won't be getting to us today?"

"It doesn't look like it, Mercer. I'm sorry. I know the situation is dire. I assure you that we are doing everything we can, though. Are you guys doing okay?"

She glanced at Derek. She remembered seeing William with those gunman. Remembered the bobcat near her cave. Remembered the mudslide and all of the aches and pains she now had as a result.

"We are hanging in," she finally said. "But we'll definitely be happy when we're able to get out of here."

"The rain is supposed to pass this afternoon. After that, I'm hoping we will be able to get to you. Maybe first thing in the morning."

"Thanks, Hendrix. I appreciate that."

"Take care of yourself, Mercer."

As she lowered the radio, she glanced at Derek again. How much more of this could they take? She wasn't sure. But their limits were about to be tested.

Derek kept listening to the radio. Kept waiting for the gunman to come over the line with another threat. Five minutes after Autumn ended her call with Hendrix, there was still nothing.

Instead, his mind went back to the conversation he'd had with Autumn earlier. She said she was happy that they had met, too. That sent a wave of delight over him. Maybe something good could come out of this situation. He would be a lucky man to have someone like Autumn by his side.

Derek glanced over at Autumn again and saw her flinch.

"You're still in pain," he muttered.

He saw the discomfort written on her face. But he tried not to push too hard. But seeing that cut…that couldn't feel good.

"I'll be okay," she insisted.

"If you don't feel like walking, we can stay here for longer."

She let out a slow breath and glanced around. "It is tempting. I was really hoping that backup would be here.

I'm afraid if we go back to that cave, we're going to need to stay there. I don't know if I can manage another trip back this way. I need food. And my leg hurts."

He nodded, knowing that they were both reaching the ends of their ropes.

"We can stay here as long as you need. You think we're safe from those men?"

"I haven't heard them. I've been listening. But we would still be wise to keep our eyes open. The last thing we need is to be ambushed."

"Let me walk to the top of that mountain and see if I can spot anybody. How does that sound?"

"Seems like a good idea."

He patted her knee before climbing to the top of the ridge. From there, he should be able to see what was going on around them.

With the storms that had come through, many of the trees had lost their leaves. That didn't help Derek and Autumn when they needed to hide, but it did help when it came to surveillance.

He scanned everything around them. On an ordinary day, he would be awestruck by the beauty surrounding him. But right now, all of this just felt like a big trap they were unable to escape.

First scan, he saw nothing.

He almost walked back down to Autumn, but he paused. He would look one more time just to be certain.

As he did, he saw something move to the west.

His muscles tensed. Was that what he thought it was?

He ducked behind a tree, just to be certain.

It was.

Two men walked their way. They were at least five hundred feet away, probably. That didn't leave them much time to hide.

He had to get back to Autumn, and he had to get back to her now.

THIRTEEN

Autumn looked up as she heard quick footsteps headed her way.

It was Derek, and his motions looked urgent. She knew that something was wrong. What had he seen?

"They're coming our way," he said. "We need to find somewhere to hide."

Though her entire body ached, she knew she was going to have to put that aside. Her adrenaline would get her through this. At least, she hoped it would.

She pushed herself up from the boulder. She'd been afraid that those gunmen may have heard that mudslide and come to find out what it was. It looked like her fears were confirmed.

"We could go to the other side of the ridge," Derek said. "Maybe there's somewhere we can hide out of sight over there. I saw an outcropping of boulders earlier."

"I think it's worth a shot. Maybe they won't go over that way."

Derek took her hand. "I'll help you."

She couldn't deny the flash of warmth that rushed through her at his touch. Who would've ever thought that a circumstance like this could have brought about such strong feelings? But it had.

However, this was not the time to think about warm, fuzzy feelings.

With Derek's help, she and Sherlock scaled the top of the ridge. They climbed over to the other side and found the outcropping of boulders he'd mentioned. There was just enough space for them to squeeze in between and to duck down low.

And they were just in time.

Voices floated with the wind.

The men were definitely getting close. In fact, it sounded like they were walking to the top of the ridge themselves to survey everything down below.

"Look at that mudslide," one of them said. "Sure wouldn't want to be caught in that."

Autumn ducked down lower, praying they wouldn't be found as she hugged Sherlock to her chest and whispered for him to be quiet.

"I wouldn't want be caught in it, but I wouldn't mind if those two we're chasing were. And their dog, too."

The men chuckled. Just hearing the sound in the conversation made Autumn bristle. Despite that, she remained down low and out of sight. One mistake could mess up everything for them.

"Do you think Foxglove is going to let us stop looking?"

"Not until he gets what he wants. But he's threatening that tonight will be the night."

"The night for what?"

"The night that we kill this William guy. He's nothing but dead weight at this point. And he didn't carry through with his end of the bargain."

What in the world were they talking about?

Autumn and Derek exchanged a look.

Footsteps came closer, and Autumn sank even lower.

Derek rested his hand on her knee, as if trying to offer her a moment of comfort.

She appreciated knowing she wasn't in this alone.

"I don't see them anywhere over here," one of them said. "Who knows where they are by now?"

"Apparently, they're still on this mountain," the other said. "Foxglove heard it on the radio. They're not getting off anytime soon."

"We better find them today then, otherwise our whole plan will be ruined."

"Let's keep looking. Maybe they're back there by the ridge where Frank fell, God rest his soul."

"Do you think he survived that fall?"

"I don't think there's any way he did. Foxglove keeps on talking about how it's the fault of that ranger and William's brother. I think it made him even more determined than ever to find them and make them pay."

"I, for one, am just ready to get out of here. This is a sopping wet, cold, awful place. I'm ready to get back home. I just hope all of this is worth it."

"Hopefully, in the end, it will be. In the end when we're rich."

They both chuckled.

Autumn and Derek exchanged a glance.

These men weren't going to give up, were they?

Derek waited until he was sure the men were gone before he said anything. "Autumn, if we don't act soon, they're going to kill William."

"It doesn't sound like this has anything to do with you, like we suspected. This has something to do with money. Maybe they want that cash that your brother was carrying?"

"If they had wanted the cash, I think William would

have just given it to him. My guess is that they want something bigger."

"Would your brother have that?"

"My brother runs a hedge fund. Ten thousand is nothing for him."

Autumn's gaze froze with that thought. "So maybe these men grabbed your brother, hoping to get a large payout from one of his investments. They could've even known who he was and followed him out here just to do that."

"I'm not sure my brother would just hand something like that over, though."

"He might be getting desperate. But I don't like the way the conversation went. It does sound like they are about to take drastic action."

"That's what I thought, too. But how do we help him?"

She let out a slow breath. "Maybe we can come up with a plan ourselves. It won't be ideal. It will be risky. It will be dangerous. But do we have any other choice right now?"

He squeezed her hand. "I don't want to put you in the middle of this."

"I appreciate that. But I am in the middle of this one way or another, whether I like it or not."

Just then her radio crackled.

Both of them froze.

Was this the bad guys? Were they contacting them again to threaten them?

Instead, they heard Hendrix's voice across the line. "Ranger Mercer?"

"I'm here. What's going on?"

"I just ran the plates on that car you saw in the lot. I'm sorry it took so long."

"It's standard procedure to send in a form recording the cars in the lots," Autumn explained. "It helps in case there's ever a missing person's report, among other things."

It made sense, Derek mused.

"What's up?" Autumn said into the radio.

"This is worse than I thought it would be. Those plates belong to Samuel Foxglove."

Foxglove? That was the name those men had used. "That name doesn't mean anything to me."

"He's known for being involved in the weapons trade," Hendrix said. "If you're stuck in the woods with him, then you are in trouble. He's a very dangerous man."

Autumn glanced at Derek. Neither needed to say a word to realize the implications of his statements.

"You need to stay away from them until help can get there."

"Do you have a description of him?" Autumn asked.

"He's six feet tall, dark hair and eyes, a scar across his cheek."

That was definitely the man they'd seen earlier.

"Do you understand that you need to stay away, Ranger Mercer?" Hendrix asked.

"I understand. Over and out."

Autumn studied Derek. He felt her eyes on him.

"Why would your brother be mixed up with Samuel Foxglove?" she asked.

Derek shook his head. "I have absolutely no idea."

"If this man is as dangerous as Hendrix says he is, then your brother really is in big trouble."

That was right. His brother needed help.

But Autumn had just told Hendrix that they would stay away until backup got there.

Derek wished they *could* stay away. But he wasn't sure they had any other choice but to get involved.

At least, *he* didn't have any other choice.

He needed to come up with a plan before those men killed William.

* * *

Autumn didn't have to know Derek well to know that his mind was racing.

She didn't have any brothers or sisters, but she could imagine that, if she did, she'd do everything in her power to help them in a situation like this. That had to be what Derek was thinking also.

She shifted her leg, wishing she hadn't gotten hurt. She could still move, but everything was going to be a little bit harder now. Their bodies were wearing down after being out here in the wilderness for so long.

Her mind raced through what Hendrix had told her. *Samuel Foxglove. Dangerous. Stay back.*

She understood all of those things. She knew the implications of the situation that they were in. It could have a very bad ending.

She had to be smart. She had to use her head. But she couldn't completely ignore her heart, either.

"I've gotta go back and help William before they kill him," Derek finally said, his head falling back against the rock behind him.

"I know," Autumn said.

He did a double take at her.

"You know?" Surprise laced his voice.

Autumn nodded. "I'm not sure that help is going to be here in time."

He shook his head. "From what that other ranger told you, it won't be."

"Let's think this through," she said. "If we were to attempt to rescue William, what would it look like?"

He let out a long breath. "I've been trying to think it through, to come up with some type of plan. I keep on trying to think like the criminals that I put behind bars.

I keep asking myself what they would do if they wanted something bad enough."

"And what did you come up with?"

He shrugged. "At first, I thought maybe we could wait until these guys were sleeping and cut a hole in the back of the tent."

"Like a bank robbery?"

He let out a soft chuckle. "Maybe. This is a terrible idea. The other men could wake up and…"

"I can see where you're going with that, but I do think we need to keep thinking about other possibilities here."

He turned toward her. "Did you have any ideas? Not that I expect you to be involved with this."

She grabbed his hand and squeezed it. "I'm involved with this whether I want to be or not."

Their gazes caught. "I don't want to see you get hurt, Autumn. I know we haven't known each other that long, but…"

She squeezed his hand. "I know. I feel it, too."

He wiped a tear from her cheek, a tear she hadn't even known was there.

"You're so beautiful," he whispered. "On the inside and out. I've never met somebody as brave and steadfast as you are."

Her heart leaped into her throat when she heard the sincerity in his words.

Slowly, Derek leaned forward, and their lips met in a soft kiss. For just a minute, all their problems disappeared and were replaced with bliss.

As he pulled away, Autumn felt a soft smile tug at the corner of his mouth. "Maybe we could try that again sometime when I'm not covered in mud and after I've gotten some sleep."

He let out a chuckle, his forehead touching hers. "That seems like a good idea."

They remained there a moment, each enjoying the bond they'd just shared.

But Autumn knew they had other things they had to think about. She pulled back, instantly missing his warmth.

She cleared her throat as she looked up at him. "I guess we really should keep brainstorming some ways to get William back. It's going to be nightfall soon, and that's probably going to be the best time to act."

Derek nodded, seeming hesitant to let her go. "I think you're right. Let's start brainstorming."

But Autumn knew she'd be thinking about that kiss for a long time.

FOURTEEN

Two hours later, Derek and Autumn had a plan.

As they'd sat in the outcropping of boulders, they'd talked through nearly every possibility they could think of.

One idea had risen above the rest. They had very few choices right now. But they might have come up with a plan that would work.

As a moment of silence fell, he glanced at Autumn. She leaned against the rocks, her eyes closed, and rubbed Sherlock's fur. The dog sat beside her, his eyes still open as if on the lookout for trouble.

Autumn looked tired. Exhausted.

They'd been able to get a little bit of rest in the outcropping of boulders. They were going to need their energy tonight.

Derek worried about her. He continued to insist that she could stay here and that he could act on this plan himself. But Autumn didn't want anything to do with that.

She kept saying that he needed a wingman, and Derek knew, in an ideal situation, that would be true. Nothing about this situation was ideal, however.

He'd spent some time scavenging the area, and he'd been able to come across an old rope. Some climbers must have used it. It hadn't been washed away by the rainwaters because it was wedged between two boulders. They would be able to use this to enact their plan this evening.

They'd drunk some water and eaten some energy bars and beef jerky, sharing all of that with Sherlock in the process.

As soon as the sun began to set, Autumn glanced at him. "You ready to head out?"

He nodded. "I guess this is as good a time as ever."

He helped her to her feet, and they began their trek toward William.

"So does the name Samuel Foxglove ring any bells yet?" Autumn asked, glancing up at him in curiosity.

"No, it doesn't."

"Do you think your brother got wrapped up in something involving weapons smuggling?"

Derek shrugged. It had been all he had been able to think about as well. "I suppose it's a possibility. The more I think about it, the more I realize that finding that cash along with the phone and the other objects in his backpack… William must have had something else in mind when he came out here. I had no idea or I never would have been a part of it."

Autumn nodded, moving a little bit slower than usual. Still, they needed to keep their energy up by maintaining a slower pace. There was no hurry to get there. They weren't going to do anything until it was dark.

Even then, they knew their plan was risky. But out of all the options they had come up with, this was the best plan of them all.

But something else had changed in Autumn also, Derek realized. She seemed more distant. More cautious.

Was it because she was in pain from her fall?

Or was it because he had kissed her?

Maybe it hadn't been the right move. But it had definitely felt right at the time.

Derek would have to worry about that later. Right now, he needed to focus on survival.

He prayed this plan didn't get them all killed.

As she walked down the mountainside, Autumn couldn't stop thinking about that kiss she and Derek had shared earlier.

It had been that blissful. A pleasant surprise in the middle of a not-so-pleasant situation.

But then reality had hit her.

She couldn't bear the thought of falling for someone and then losing them again.

Losing Kevin had nearly wrecked her. And now Autumn was putting herself into a situation where she was falling for a man in the midst of a dangerous, life-threatening situation.

She couldn't do this again. She had to put some distance between herself and Derek. It was better to feel the pain now than it would be later, after her feelings grew even more. After she got used to being around him more. After she became dependent on him as a companion.

Her chest squeezed with sadness at the thought.

She needed to stay focused. To think about their plan. These feelings right now would distract her. Could make her not as sharp or on top of things.

She wasn't confident that her and Derek's plan was going to work.

But it was all they had, she mused as she climbed up a steep incline. Her muscles strained with the action, but she pushed forward. Despite the cold. Despite the dampness. Despite the pain.

Out of all the options she and Derek had discussed, this

had been the one that made the most sense given their situation and resources.

A flutter of nerves still lingered inside her. So much could go wrong. Autumn dreaded the thought of facing those gunmen, especially in her current weakened state.

She pushed back some thick foliage, trying to watch her step as the darkness grew deeper.

What if it was still a couple days until rescuers could get to them? They were going to be stuck out here with these men, and they couldn't simply be sitting ducks. They needed to be proactive.

Autumn also knew if this plan worked, that there would still be more obstacles to face. Starting with the fact that William could barely walk. At least, that was the case last they knew.

She continued to lift up prayers for this situation.

Finally, the three of them reached the campsite of the gunmen. They paused a safe distance away so they wouldn't be discovered.

Nightfall was upon them and worked in their favor right now. Autumn could be thankful for that, at least.

She lingered behind a tree and watched as the three men were sitting around the campfire. William was out there also, but he leaned against a tree, almost appearing like he couldn't even hold himself up. Based on his hunched body, the bandage on his arm and leg, and his sunken eyes, he wasn't doing well.

Meanwhile, the other three men sat around together, looking like they were just friends on a trip together as they laughed and drank.

Just what were they planning? It was obvious by the conversation she and Derek had overheard earlier that the men had planned on killing William tonight. To look at them now, Autumn wouldn't have guessed that.

Something didn't make sense.

She leaned toward Derek. "I'm going to get a little closer. Stay here."

His eyes widened, but he nodded as if he trusted her. "Be careful."

"I will be." Remaining low, Autumn crept close enough to hear more of their conversation. She needed to know exactly what she was getting into. She couldn't lead everyone into an ambush.

"We need to figure this out before the roads open back up," Foxglove said. "When that happens, there's going to be law enforcement all over this area."

"How much time do you think we have?" the man with his arm in a sling asked.

"My guess? Less than forty-eight hours."

"You going to tell us where that money is?" Foxglove asked, turning to William.

"I told you. I hid it in my backpack behind some rocks. But it was gone when we got back there. I don't know what happened."

"He's sticking to his story," Foxglove said.

"That's because it's the truth!" William's voice rose with emotion.

"We have other means of getting what we need," Foxglove continued. "Just wait."

"Your beef is with me. Leave my brother out of this."

"It's too late for that." The third man let out a deep, menacing chuckle.

What did that mean? Autumn wondered. What else was going on here?

Autumn didn't like the sound of this. Exactly what kind of situation were they putting themselves in? Part of her wanted to run, to forget about this.

Then she remembered Derek. She had to do whatever

she could to help him. It was clear that these men weren't going to wait until the conditions cleared and backup was able to come and help Autumn out.

If they didn't act soon, William would die.

As soon as darkness completely surrounded them and the men had disappeared inside their tents, Derek and Autumn decided it was safe enough to act.

Derek was surprised that no one had been left outside to guard everything. But that would work in their favor, so he wasn't complaining.

Instead, he and Autumn looked at each other and nodded.

It was time to put their plan in place. He only prayed that everything worked out the way it was supposed to.

Moving carefully, they walked to the opposite side of the camp. They collected as many sticks and branches as they could and leaned them against each other, almost like a tepee.

They kept adding to the arrangement for as long as they could, knowing that the bigger they could build it, the more effective it would be. Even Sherlock helped, carrying sticks in his mouth toward the structure.

They had to be careful to be quiet, otherwise they would draw attention to themselves and everything would be ruined.

Finally, the construction was set in place. Autumn tied a rope around one of the sticks, and they dragged the cord through the woods as far as they could.

Autumn turned to Derek. "You're sure you're up for this?"

He'd be lying if he said he wasn't a little anxious about how everything would play out. But this was still their best bet.

"I've got this," he told her.

She stared at him another moment before nodding and taking a step back. "I'll be waiting on the other side of the camp."

"I'll get there as soon as I can."

She stared at him one more moment before nodding. Then she and Sherlock walked away.

When Derek was sure they were a safe enough distance from him, he looked down at the rope in his hands. As soon as he pulled on this, everything would be set in place. There would be no going back.

Maybe he should have tried to do all this without Autumn. But he knew there was no way she wasn't going to help. Even if he had tried to sneak off to do this on his own, she would have found him. Certainly, she knew exactly where he would have been heading.

But that didn't bring him very much comfort. The way to solve this problem wasn't by getting more people hurt.

Despite that, he knew that their plan was solid. The only potential hiccup he could see was the fact that his brother could hardly walk. It was going to be much harder to escape with him for that reason.

The good news was they didn't plan on going too far. They would take William back to that outcropping of boulders. Derek hoped that they could stay there until help arrived. The covering was perfect for them, just out of sight to anybody who might be looking.

He swallowed hard and looked down at the rope one more time.

It was now or never.

He let out his breath and then tugged on it.

A loud crash sounded in the distance as the sticks hit the ground.

This was it.

Derek had to move.

As he heard the men scrambling from their tents, he ran back toward Autumn.

He only paused long enough to double-check that the men had run toward the commotion.

All three of them.

This was his chance to grab William and make a run for it.

FIFTEEN

Autumn remained at her perch and watched everything play out.

So far, everything was going according to plan.

The tepee of sticks had fallen, causing a loud enough crash to get the men's attention.

All three of them had hurried from their tents to see what had happened.

That meant that they'd left William alone.

The unknown right now was how long they would stay gone.

Derek and Autumn had built that stack of sticks far enough away that it would take a considerable amount of time to go check things out. But if the men returned to their camp immediately…that could lead to trouble.

From her position, she watched as Derek darted toward the tent where William was staying. She held her breath, watching as he disappeared inside.

Please, Lord…

Part of her wished she could go help, but she knew she'd only get in the way right now. It was best if she remained on lookout, with her gun drawn.

Like she was now.

First sign of trouble, she'd fire a warning shot. If the men persisted, she would take aim at them.

They couldn't take any unnecessary chances out here.

Some people would say that even attempting to rescue William was an unnecessary chance. But they had to do whatever they could.

Autumn held her breath, watching and waiting.

She could only imagine Derek waking up his brother, trying to get him on his feet so they could get away.

His injury might be one of the biggest obstacles that they had to overcome.

Her gaze scanned the perimeter again.

She saw nothing. No one.

Hopefully, it would remain that way for at least ten or fifteen more minutes.

That's how much time they needed just to get William and to get away from here.

Finally, she saw Derek and William emerge. Derek had his arm around his brother, and William's face was scrunched in obvious pain.

This wasn't going to be easy for him, but there was no other way.

The two of them hurried toward Autumn. As soon as they reached her, she'd help escort them away. Right now, she was just acting as security.

Again, she scanned everything around them.

Still nothing.

She continued to pray that it would stay that way.

Sherlock let out a little whine beside her, almost as if he agreed with her silent assessment. That dog always seemed to read her thoughts.

Finally, Derek and William reached her.

Her heart soared with a moment of victory.

But she couldn't celebrate for too long. They had to move.

"Glad you guys made it." She nodded toward the distance. "We've got to get going. Now."

Derek had never been so happy to see his brother. William hadn't been sleeping when he had gone into the tent. No, he was sitting up, almost as if waiting for more trouble to find him.

Then his face had crashed with relief when he'd spotted Derek.

The two of them hadn't had a chance for a reunion. They had to keep moving.

Helping his brother was even harder than Derek had anticipated. Not only was his leg broken, but those men had shot him in the arm. Though the bullet had only skimmed his skin—leaving that blood they'd found earlier—it was obviously painful for William if anything touched that area.

His brother was also a big guy, and though Derek could handle his weight, it made moving through the forest even more cumbersome.

It didn't matter. They just had to get away from these guys before they were caught.

"I'm Autumn." She glanced at William before her gaze traveled down to his leg. "Feeling okay?"

William shook his head. "No. I got a fever yesterday. I know enough to know that's not good."

No, it wasn't, Derek mused. That probably meant that infection was setting in. If his brother didn't get medical help soon, then he really was going to be in trouble.

Derek let out another grunt as he helped his brother up a rock. Autumn slipped an arm around him also to help out.

But her gaze still remained focused on everything around them. They had to be careful here.

Derek glanced back one more time.

Enough time had passed that those gunmen should be returning to their camp soon. Certainly they'd realized they'd been duped. They weren't going to be happy when they found out about it.

That was another reason why Derek and his companions had to continue to make good time here.

"How did you guys find me?" William asked, his voice ragged, like he was out of breath. A thin sheen of sweat covered his skin, and his gaze looked hollow.

"Sherlock helped." Autumn glanced down at her dog. "But these men have also been on our trail for the past couple days. Do you know who they are?"

"Samuel Foxglove." His brother's face scrunched with either pain or disgust—or both.

"Listen, save your breath," Derek said. "We'll talk more when we get to our safe location."

"Safe location?"

"It's not much," Autumn said. "But we have somewhere that should hold us over until backup arrives."

"I was hoping backup might already be here." William let out a moan as they continued to move through the forest.

"The roads are washed out," Derek said. "The storm did a number on the area, and they're having trouble getting anybody else out here."

William let out a groan. "That's not what I want to hear."

"Believe me, it's not what any of us wanted to hear," Autumn said. "We've got to keep moving."

It seemed the farther they went, the heavier his brother became. William couldn't put any weight at all onto his foot, which meant he was hopping between every other step. He also used Derek and Autumn as crutches.

This was going to be a long and slow way to travel. But they had no other choice right now. Perhaps if they'd had more time and resources, they could have made some type of device to help pull him.

But it was too late for that now.

They just had to move.

Autumn didn't like any of this. She'd known it was going to be difficult to rescue William. But they were moving entirely too slowly.

Though she tried to help, she also needed to keep her eyes and ears open for any signs of trouble. Between trying to assist William and navigating this mountain, she glanced around.

So far, she had seen nothing.

But certainly those men had gotten back to the camp by now. Certainly, they'd realized that William was not there anymore. At any time now, they were going to start coming after them.

Autumn knew the men would be able to move faster than they could. That was going to be a problem.

There was no time to lose.

By her estimations, they had at least another half a mile until they reached their temporary shelter.

That was their best bet at this point.

But she worried if they were going to be able to make it or not.

At least the darkness was their friend.

She knew this area better than almost anyone. Even in this blinding darkness, she had a general idea of where they needed to go.

Those men? They could very well get lost out here.

Was it wrong to hope that they might?

William let out another grunt.

Autumn's heart pounded with compassion. She knew this couldn't be easy for him.

But there would be time to talk to him later.

Right now, they just had to move. The thick trees and steep landscape didn't make it easy, nor did the nighttime that hung around them.

She glanced behind her again, looking for any signs of trouble.

Still nothing.

Besides, Sherlock would let her know if someone approached.

That didn't stop the anxiety from knitting itself in her back muscles.

William let out another grunt. He wasn't doing well. His face looked pale. His breathing was too shallow.

Maybe all of this was a bad idea.

Still, Autumn had known they couldn't leave the man there to die.

"Do we need to stop?" she asked as she felt William's weight pressing on her.

"No," William said through gritted teeth. "I can keep going."

Autumn exchanged a look with Derek. He was obviously worried, too. Tension hardened his jaw.

They continued forward, but with every step, Autumn's anxiety grew.

Why didn't she hear those men yet? They should be following after them by now. Certainly, they'd realized what the plan had been.

That uncomfortable feeling grew in her yet again.

As if Sherlock could read her thoughts, he paused and let out a low growl.

Something was wrong.

Danger was near.

Derek cast her another glance, as if he sensed it also.

They froze, and Autumn held out her gun, ready to act. But before she could, she heard a click.

And another.

Then another.

"Put your gun down," someone said. "We have you surrounded. One wrong move, and we will shoot."

Autumn knew better than to argue. She slowly lowered her weapon to the ground and waited for whatever was about to happen.

SIXTEEN

Derek sucked in a quick breath. He wanted to glance at Autumn, but he already knew how she would look.

Full of apprehension.

Just like he felt.

How had those men found them? And what would they do with them now?

They had seemed so close to freedom.

Despair threatened to consume him, but he couldn't let it.

Autumn raised her hands in the air. "Don't shoot."

Three men, all armed, stepped out of the darkness.

Foxglove stepped closer to Derek, leering in his face. "You really thought you were going to get away with your little plan?"

Derek raised his chin. "As a matter of fact, yes, I did."

"It's a good thing that we are smarter than you, then. As soon as we saw that wood, we knew something was up. We're not as dumb as you think we are."

"We never said you were dumb," Derek said. "Why don't you just let us go? We could pretend like this never happened."

He knew it was a long shot, but it seemed worth a try.

Foxglove let out a deep, throaty chuckle. "I'm afraid that's not possible. Not until we get what we want."

Derek glanced at his brother, wondering exactly what kind of trouble he'd gotten himself into.

Then he briefly closed his eyes and lifted a prayer that they weren't all going to die right now. They had come this far. They couldn't be defeated now.

"Start moving," Foxglove said. "You can help your brother walk. But one wrong move, and I'm going to pull this trigger." He turned to face Autumn. "And I'm going to start with her."

Derek glanced at Autumn and saw her face looked paler.

And suddenly he knew that this was all a bad, bad idea. He should have never dragged her into this.

Because he would never forgive himself if something happened to her.

This wasn't the way things were supposed to work out, Autumn mused.

She kept one hand on Sherlock's leash and the other raised in the air as the gunmen led them away.

They had been so close to freedom. So close.

How had those men sneaked up on them without them ever hearing a thing?

It didn't matter now. All that mattered was that it was done.

Now she and Derek had to figure out what they were going to do next.

It was clear that rescuing William was going to be even more difficult than she and Derek had anticipated. He just wasn't in any shape to walk through these mountains.

If they could survive until tomorrow morning, maybe her fellow rangers would get here in time. But in the meantime...they needed to figure out how to stay alive.

As they continued through the woods, the man shoved Autumn. Sherlock growled, showing his teeth and threatening to protect Autumn.

"It's okay, boy," she muttered, keeping her tone calm.

The last thing she wanted was for Sherlock to try to protect her and for her dog to get hurt in the process. She would do whatever it took to keep her canine safe. He'd do the same for her.

"You weren't ever supposed to be involved in this," Foxglove said.

Autumn knew he was talking to her.

"Funny you said that," Autumn said. "Because you guys weren't supposed to be out here on park property doing anything illegal."

The man chuckled, as if breaking the law amused him. "You're feisty. I like that."

"Let her go," Derek muttered. "It's like you said. She has nothing to do with this."

"I can see he's got a soft spot for you," Foxglove said, mischief rising in his tone. "That will be good to keep in mind."

Autumn felt the tension pull across her chest. It seemed like with every minute that passed, the situation just got worse. Maybe they shouldn't have ever attempted this rescue. Then again, what choice had they really had?

Finally, they reached the camp. Foxglove shoved Autumn forward again, as if to quicken her steps. The thrust threw her off balance, but she caught herself before hitting the ground.

When she looked up at Derek, she saw the anger brewing in his eyes.

She shook her head subtly, letting him know that she was okay and that he shouldn't react. That's what these guys wanted. They wanted an excuse to go ballistic on them. She and Derek couldn't let that happen, though.

"Tie them up to these trees," Foxglove barked. "They obviously can't be trusted."

The men began securing Derek, then Autumn, with some old rope that they wound around their midsections. They attached Sherlock's leash to a hook on another tree and then tied up William to a tree on the other side of the camp.

Autumn watched carefully, trying to see what their next move would be. Would they begin to interrogate them right here, right now? What kind of information did they even want to know?

She remained quiet, not wanting to provoke anyone. The best thing she could do right now was to try to stay under the radar. At least until she got her feet back under her.

She watched as the men huddled together on the side of the camp, murmuring things to each other that she couldn't make out. The man with his arm in a sling was apparently Whitaker, and the third man went by Montgomery.

She made mental notes in case she needed to know that later, after they were rescued.

Because she had to hold on to hope that they would be rescued.

A few minutes later, the trio disbanded, and Foxglove strode toward Derek.

"Where is it?" he demanded.

"Where is what?" Derek asked.

Could they be talking about the ten thousand that had been found in the backpack? That was the only thing that made sense to Autumn. But there was clearly more to this story.

"Your brother owes us some money." Foxglove practically spat out the words. "It's missing. Did you take it with you?"

"I didn't steal any money from my brother, if that's what you're asking," Derek said.

Foxglove pointed his gun at Derek. "But do you know where it is?"

"He doesn't know anything about it." William rushed before his voice became strained. His face scrunched with pain. "It's what I've been telling you. Just let him go."

"I wouldn't have had to capture him at all if you'd give me back the money that's mine," Foxglove said.

"The money you owe him?" Derek repeated, staring at his brother.

William let out a breath and lowered his chin toward his chest. "It's a long story."

"William…what did you do?" Disappointment rang through Derek's voice.

Foxglove chuckled as he paced in front of them. "You really don't know, do you?"

"I have no idea."

"Your brother got into some gambling debt. He desperately needed some money, so he made a deal with me."

"What kind of deal did he make, exactly?" Derek's gaze went to William, and Autumn saw the questions in his eyes. This was all a shock to Derek.

"He helped us set up an account for our weapons trading business. Meanwhile, we paid off his debt. Win-win. Until he disappeared with some of our cash."

Autumn processed everything that was being said. This didn't look good. What was William thinking when he got tied up with these guys?

It didn't matter right now. What was done was done.

Derek listened as Foxglove addressed everyone like a militant leader planning a coup.

"First thing in the morning, we're going to find that

money. Until we do, I'm going start picking people off one by one." Foxglove stared at all of them, his gaze unrelenting. "In the meantime, I hope you guys all try to get some sleep. It's going to be a long day tomorrow. At least, for some of you it will be."

He let out a heartless laugh, one that made it clear that human life meant nothing to him.

Derek glanced at Autumn and then at William. How were they going to get out of this one?

He wasn't sure. They were dealing with some dangerous men here.

Now that he'd had a closer look at Foxglove, he realized he had seen the man before.

He and his brother had stopped at a café on the way here. As Derek had paid, he'd seen a man watching him from across the dining area.

Derek hadn't thought much of it. He'd assumed that the man was a local and had noticed a new face in the area.

But these guys had followed them here. They had followed them through the wilderness, all in a quest to get this money from William. The first chance they had to grab his brother, they'd obviously done that.

What a nightmare.

After Foxglove finished his tyrannical speech, he and his men disappeared into the woods for a moment, talking quietly between themselves. Derek didn't know how long it would be until they were back.

The night was cold and damp. Animals scampered in the background. The wind rustled the leaves. Tree branches clacked together.

When Derek was sure the men weren't listening, he called across the campsite to his brother. "William."

His brother's weary eyes met his, his head barely raising up. "I'm sorry, man. I never meant to get you involved with this."

"What's going on?" Derek continued. He needed some answers. They couldn't wait any longer.

"What Foxglove said was true." William's voice sounded breathless, ragged and lined with pain. "I had big gambling debts. These guys promised to help me. All I had to do was to set up an account for them so they could funnel their money there without penalty. In return, they let me borrow fifty thousand dollars."

"We found some money at the bottom of your backpack. Is that what they're talking about?"

"No, that money was so I could escape. But I tried to give it to them as a good faith promise. When I got back to the campsite with them to retrieve it, my bag was gone."

"The water must have washed it downstream."

"I figured something like that must have happened. It was the only thing that made sense."

"Why didn't you tell me any of this before we came out here?" Derek asked, disappointment rippling through him. "Maybe I could have helped you out before you had to turn to illegal means."

"I didn't know what else to do. I didn't want to tell you. I knew you'd be upset."

"So you brought me out here basically to say goodbye? Then you were going to take off?" Derek wouldn't put a lot past William, but this shocked even Derek. He'd thought his brother was better than this.

"I know how it probably sounds, but it was all I knew to do. I didn't want to totally disappear without ever speaking to you again."

"That money wouldn't have lasted you very long." Certainly, his brother knew that. He would need access to more funds than that if he wanted to start a new life. And he had to know these guys were going to come after him.

William shrugged. "I was doing my best to get by. I didn't know what else to do. I panicked."

"Why haven't they killed you yet? Why didn't you just tell them?" Something wasn't adding up in Derek's mind. Was he missing something still?

"Like I said, I told them I had some cash in the backpack, but then the bag disappeared. They didn't believe me. The only reason they're keeping me alive is because they think I know where the money is."

"I know where that ten thousand dollars is," Derek said.

William's eyes lit with hope. "Then you've got to tell them."

Derek feared if he did tell them that information, they would all end up dead anyway.

SEVENTEEN

Autumn listened to the conversation between Derek and William, knowing she needed to stay out of it. This was between the two of them—for now.

As a moment of silence fell, her radio crackled. A moment later, Hendrix's voice came on the line. "Ranger Mercer? Are you there?"

Hope trickled inside her.

She stretched her arm, wondering if she could somehow reach the device. It was on a log, only a couple feet away. Or maybe her foot could kick it...

Almost as if he'd been lingering close to eavesdrop, Foxglove appeared from the woods and glowered down at her. He held a gun in his hands, the end pointed at her.

She glanced back at Derek then at Foxglove again. She knew that one wrong move, and Foxglove would pull that trigger. One of them would end up dead.

"Answer it," Foxglove growled as he picked up the device. "But make one mention of what's going on here, there will be casualties."

Tension snaked up her spine at his ominous-sounding words. Before she could think too much, Foxglove held it to her mouth and pressed the button there.

Her throat burned as she said, "This is Ranger Mercer."

"Good to hear your voice. You doing okay?"

Autumn glanced at Foxglove again, feeling his burning gaze on bearing down on her. "Doing fine."

"The roads are still washed out coming from the west. But the good news is I think we can get a team in coming from the east."

She glanced at Foxglove again, waiting for his indication as to what she should say next.

"Tell him you're fine and that there's no hurry," he whispered.

"He's not going to believe that," Autumn said. "He already knows that there's somebody out here with a broken leg. He knows that you're out here, too."

His nostrils flared. "Tell him that William has passed away and you haven't had any more trouble. That there's no hurry."

Autumn continued to stare at him, apprehension racing through her blood. She repeated, "He's never going to believe that."

Foxglove leaned closer until he was in her face, his rancid breath flooding her cheeks. "Then make him believe it."

She sucked in a deep breath, trying to quickly formulate her thoughts. She would never forgive herself if she made a wrong move that resulted in somebody getting hurt. She was going to have to play by Foxglove's rules right now.

Autumn nodded, and Foxglove squeezed the button on the radio again.

She swallowed hard before saying, "I'm sorry to tell you that the man we were looking for has been found. He didn't make it."

William's face went pale as he heard those words being said out loud.

"I'm sorry to hear that," Hendrix said. "Where is your

location? We'll still get a team in there to get you out and to recover his body."

Autumn glanced around, trying to figure out what to tell him exactly. Before she spoke, she saw Foxglove's raised gun point toward Derek.

Her throat tightened even more.

"I know you have a lot of other things going on," she finally said. "We'll be fine here for a little while longer. We have food and shelter. Take care of whatever you need to. I know there are a lot of people out there who need help."

"I can't argue with that. What about the gunman you mentioned? Any updates on that situation?"

Autumn swallowed hard as she stared at Foxglove. "I haven't heard from them. They must have left."

"That's good news, at least. Listen, our incident report list is a mile long," Hendrix said. "But we'll get to you as soon as we can."

"Like I said, I'm doing fine. Don't worry about me right now. We'll huddle down until help arrives." It pained her for the words to leave her lips. Help seemed so close, and she was sending it away.

"When we get closer, I'll radio you so we can find out your exact location. Sound good?"

"Sounds like a plan. Thanks, Hendrix."

As soon as the radio conversation ended, Foxglove put the radio back on the ground and everyone turned to stare at him, waiting for his next instruction.

"Sounds like we'll be safe here for a little longer." Foxglove paced in front of everyone, still holding his gun. "That's a good thing. Because we're not done yet. We want our money back. The money that was stolen from us."

"I'm not sure how you think you're going to get that out here in the woods," Derek said. "Nobody has any type of internet connection to make any transfers here."

"We'll figure out a way," Foxglove said. "We always do."

Autumn shivered. She heard the pure evil in his voice. And she had no idea how they were going to get out of this situation alive.

Derek felt the tension growing in him. They were at these men's mercy, and there was nothing they could do to save themselves right now. They were literally tied to trees with no weapons and no means of escaping. Even if they somehow managed to untie themselves, there was no way to escape with William. That was clear.

Derek had to think of another plan.

He glanced around.

The men had disappeared into their tents, and William appeared to be passed out against the tree across from them. When everything was silent, Derek turned toward Autumn, anxious to talk to her privately.

Her eyes looked tired. The ponytail she'd pulled her hair into was crooked and loose. Her clothes were muddy.

But she was still a sight to behold, even in this state.

"I'm sorry I got you into all this," Derek said.

She offered an exhausted smile. "None of this is your fault. The only people that I blame for this are Samuel Foxglove and his crew."

He knew her words were true, but that didn't stop the guilt from flooding him. "What are we going to do?"

She grimaced. "I wish I knew. I'm trying to saw through this rope using the tree bark, but it's a slow process."

"I have been trying to rub it against the tree also. But even if we manage to get these ropes off…" His voice drifted. This had been all he could think about. "I was thinking, maybe you and Sherlock could run for it. I could stay here with my brother and—"

"Then they would end up killing both of you," Autumn

finished. "They've made it clear that if we make one wrong move, we're goners. I believe them."

So did Derek. But there had to be something that they could do. They couldn't just sit here.

"I still think it might be worth it for you to try to escape," Derek said. "None of this is your fault. And I know you don't blame us. But my brother stole money. That's what set all of this in motion. You don't deserve to be in the middle of it."

"Derek…" She stared at him, her eyes orbs of compassion.

"It's true." His voice cracked. "You've been a real superstar during all of this. I'd probably be dead right now if it weren't for you. But you don't deserve to be in the middle of the situation."

"Derek…" She tilted her head and frowned.

There was nothing she could say. He knew the truth.

"I need to get you free. You and Sherlock need to go. I'll handle things here and face the consequences."

Autumn didn't say anything for a moment before frowning. "I want to say you're wrong. But unless we have help, I'm not sure any of us are going to get out of this."

At least they were on the same page with that thought. Now they needed an escape plan.

"How's the rope coming?" he asked.

Her teeth clenched as her arms continued to make slight up and down motions. "I think it's getting thinner. I'm doing my best."

"Do you think Hendrix believed you when you said you didn't need his help?" Derek whispered.

She shrugged. "I don't know. He knows me pretty well, so I'm hoping he can read between the lines. But I also know the park service has a lot going on right now."

That's what Derek had assumed also. "Maybe he'll send

someone anyway. Wouldn't that be nice? To have a cavalry riding in right now?"

"Maybe. But we shouldn't plan on that. Right now, we only have ourselves."

"I agree."

Just then, Autumn's eyes widened, and she shifted. "Derek…"

"What is it?"

The next instant, the rope fell from around her body. She pulled her arms out in front of her. "I did it."

His heart leaped with hope. Maybe they would get out of this situation. "Now, can you get Sherlock?"

"I can try. I'm not leaving here without him." She stood and started toward her canine.

But before she got there, a click sounded.

"I don't know what you think you're doing," someone growled. "But I would sit back down by the tree if I were you."

Derek looked over and saw Foxglove's face come into focus. The man must have just been watching and waiting for them to make a move. And he had caught them.

The hope that Derek had growing inside him fizzled like a closing argument gone bad.

Autumn stared at Foxglove's gun. She knew without a doubt that the man wouldn't be afraid to use it. But the last thing she wanted was to be tied up to a tree again. Next time, she wouldn't be so fortunate at getting herself untied.

She was certain that they had no time to waste right now. William was fading by the moment, and, if they didn't get him medical help soon, he was going to go septic.

"Get over there," Foxglove said, pointing at the tree with his gun.

Sherlock growled, looking ready to pounce as soon as Autumn gave him the signal.

"You don't want to do this." Autumn raised her hands in the air.

"Don't tell me what I do and don't want to do."

"I'm a park ranger. If you hurt me, you'll face time in federal prison." Her voice sounded strained.

"I'm already facing time in federal prison. And if I let William off the hook, what kind of precedent will this set for other people who try to steal from me? Not a good one. He's made his bed—now he has to lie in it. Unfortunately, he dragged you two into this mess also. Stinks to be you."

"Maybe we can think of a compromise." Autumn raised her hand in the air, trying to look unassuming. She had to use whatever tactics she could think of right now.

Foxglove stepped closer. "There's no compromising here. I need to get what William took from me. It's important enough that I came all the way out here to this wet, remote, nightmarish place to make my point."

"I understand that—" Before Autumn could finish her sentence, Foxglove slapped his gun across her face.

Pain ripped through her skull, and she grasped the area of impact. Everything around her began to spin.

Sherlock snarled, his claws digging into the dirt as he tried to get to Foxglove.

"Autumn!" Derek yelled.

She looked back at him and saw him tugging against his confines. He wanted to get to her, to help.

But it was no use.

No one could help right now.

"Now, do I make myself clear?" Foxglove glowered at her. "There's no compromising. You have no say so in any of this. You're going to do it exactly like I tell you or else."

"Yeah, I get it." Autumn's hand remained on her cheek,

which now throbbed uncontrollably. She'd never been hit like that before. In all of her training to be a ranger, she'd never gotten into a scuffle.

Montgomery emerged from the darkness and took her arm. He shoved her against the tree and began wrapping the rope around her again.

"Do it tighter this time," Foxglove said. "And next time, if you get out, we're not going to have a conversation. I'm just going to shoot. Do you understand?"

Autumn nodded. She had no doubt his words were true. "Understood."

"Now, get some rest." Foxglove practically spat out the words. "Because the two of you are going to have a long day tomorrow."

"Why is that?" Autumn asked.

"Because I need a little goodwill offering that's going to assure me that William is going to be able to pay me back my money."

"What's that?" Derek asked.

"You're going to take us to get that ten thousand dollars he brought with him. After that, I'll worry about the rest of the money he owes me. Now, get your beauty rest. Because I am going to take everything you've got tomorrow."

Derek's heart throbbed in his ears. He couldn't believe the man had hit Autumn. More than anything, Derek wanted to bust out of these ropes and get to her.

But he knew that was an impossibility.

Instead, he stared at her from his confines. "Are you okay?"

She nodded, resting her head against the tree behind her. "Sorry. I was close."

"No, I'm sorry. He shouldn't have hit you like that." Anger still burned through him at the thought of it.

He watched as she closed her eyes, and he wanted nothing more than to comfort her.

But he couldn't.

He cared about her. He knew that. But Derek had sensed her pulling away earlier.

Maybe he shouldn't have kissed her. Maybe she wasn't ready for that. Or maybe she wasn't interested.

But Derek knew without a doubt that he cared about Autumn. Seeing her in pain did something to his heart. It almost brought out a primal side of him that wanted to lunge at the men and attack them.

He couldn't do that. Even if he could, it wouldn't be wise.

"What are we going to do tomorrow?" Derek whispered.

"It sounds like we have no choice but to show them where that money is."

"But the hike is treacherous," Derek reminded her.

"I know. I don't like it, either. But I don't know what other choice we have." She closed her eyes and leaned her head against the tree.

Derek could tell that she was getting tired. So was he. Everything that happened over the past couple days was catching up with them. Their bodies—and minds—were exhausted and needed to recover.

What a nightmare. Sometimes, none of this seemed real. He often prayed that it wasn't real, that he would wake up.

But that hadn't happened yet.

Dear Lord, please help this situation. Protect Autumn. Give us wisdom. Don't let our enemies win.

Derek closed his eyes. He knew he should try to get some sleep. Maybe with some rest, he would see things clearly and his reactions would be more thought out.

But there was no getting any rest out here.

Not only was it cold and damp, but there was too much on the line for him to allow himself that luxury.

An invisible weight pressed on his shoulders. He had to figure out what to do to make this situation right before someone else got hurt again.

EIGHTEEN

Autumn's face still ached as the sun began to come up. If she had a mirror, she was sure she'd see a large bruise on her jaw. It hurt every time she opened her mouth to yawn.

The good news was that she was still alive.

She wasn't sure how much longer she'd be able to say that.

Derek was right to be concerned about the hike today. It was one thing to make the trek in your right state of mind, when you've gotten sleep and when you'd eaten.

But the elements, when combined with their sleepless nights and lack of good nutrition, would be even more dangerous.

What were these men really going to do with her and Derek as soon as they had that ten thousand dollars? Would there be any need to keep them around for longer?

For that matter, Autumn was kind of surprised they hadn't tried to take William back to their vehicle so they could attempt to find a computer and he could make some type of financial transaction that way. Then again, she supposed Foxglove and his men knew that the roads had washed out.

If only she could somehow get a message to Hendrix. But she didn't know how she could do that without alerting these men to what she was doing.

She glanced over at Derek. His eyes were closed, though she doubted he was actually sleeping.

When she'd seen the concern in his gaze last night, it had done something inside her.

She reminded herself not to get attached. It was too hard to lose the people that she loved. Although she had been thoroughly impressed with the man, she knew there was a chance that both of them wouldn't be getting out of the situation alive.

She couldn't bear the thought of losing someone else that she loved.

Loved? It was too soon to say that she loved him. Of course. But the feelings she'd begun to feel for him were definitely growing, getting stronger all the time.

She needed to stop them before they went any further. Before she set herself up for heartbreak.

The sound of one of the men talking drifted through the air, and a moment later Foxglove stepped out. His men followed after.

At his instructions, they untied her, Derek and Sherlock. She held her dog back as Sherlock snarled at the man. The canine had always been a great judge of character.

"As far as I'm concerned, that dog is dead weight." Foxglove narrowed his eyes at Sherlock. "One wrong move, and I'm pulling the trigger."

Autumn leaned to the ground and put her arms around her dog, feeling a surge of protectiveness. She whispered in his ear, "It's okay, boy."

She couldn't bear the thought of anything happening to her furry companion.

Foxglove tossed each of them some water and an energy bar. "Here is your ration for the day. Drink and eat up. You're going to need your strength."

She unscrewed the water bottle and sipped. Then she cupped her hand and filled it with water for Sherlock.

"You're giving your only water for the day to your dog?" Foxglove asked, looking almost like he pitied her.

"I'm not going to let him go thirsty or hungry. I'm not that kind of person."

"If I were you, that dog would've been the first thing to go." His eyes hardened, and he shook his head.

Autumn had no doubt that he'd told the truth. The man lacked any type of moral compass. That's what made him so dangerous.

She took the energy bar and quickly read the ingredients. It looked like it would be safe to give some of this to Sherlock also.

She broke off half the bar and gave it to the dog, who gobbled it up. Then she began nibbling on the rest of it.

As she did, she glanced at Derek. His muscles looked bristled and tense as he stood nearby.

Then her gaze went to William. He was still alive, letting out little moans in his sleep.

But he wasn't doing well.

He needed medical help, and he needed it soon.

More unseen pressure mounted between her shoulders.

"You guys ready to get going?" Foxglove turned back to them, gun still in his hands.

"As if we have a choice," Derek said.

Foxglove laughed. "Now you're catching on. Do I need to remind you of the consequences here?" Foxglove grabbed Autumn's arm and pressed the gun to her temple.

She sucked in a breath. Sherlock growled at her feet, ready to launch at the man.

"Call off your dog," Foxglove said, almost as if he were testing them.

"Heel, boy," Autumn said. "Heel."

Sherlock sat back, but she could see the look in his eyes. A look that clearly said he was ready to attack as soon as Autumn gave him the signal.

Part of her wished she could do that. That she could just tell him to assault the men around her.

But all of these men had guns, and she feared Sherlock would be a casualty. She couldn't risk that.

"Let her go," Derek said, his voice tense with barely restrained emotion.

Foxglove stared at him for a moment before shoving Autumn away from him. She caught herself before she tumbled to the ground.

"I just want to make it clear what will happen if something goes wrong," Foxglove continued.

"I think you've made that abundantly clear," Derek said through clenched teeth. "If you need someone to manipulate William, use me. Not her."

Autumn felt her heart launch into her throat. His care and concern for her were touching.

A tension pulled inside her.

Part of her didn't want to get too close to the man. She wanted to put up all the boundaries that she could to protect her heart.

But the other part of her knew finding someone who would sacrifice himself for her was a rare gift. She knew she'd be foolish to let him walk away at the end of this.

She didn't have time to consider those thoughts any longer. Foxglove pushed them ahead, and they began their trek to retrieve the missing money.

* * *

Anger continued to mount inside Derek.

He wasn't one who got into fistfights. He had always preferred his battles to be of the intellectual kind.

But right now, something carnal rose inside him. He wanted nothing more than to turn all of his rage onto this man until he got his hands off of Autumn.

He reminded himself that reaction would do them no good right now. No good would come of letting his emotions get the best of him.

Autumn led them down the path, back toward the cave where they had stowed the money. Whitaker stayed behind with William.

Foxglove and Montgomery came with them. Both had their guns drawn, just in case anyone made a sudden move.

Autumn said very little as she walked through the trees in between the boulders. But Derek could tell from the way she walked and moved that she was still in pain.

She still hadn't recovered from that mudslide yesterday. The cut on her leg had been pretty bad, and Derek knew she'd hit her hip and shoulder. That, when coupled with Foxglove's attack last night…she had to be in pain. Too much pain.

What Derek wouldn't do to put himself in her place, to switch positions with her.

If only things could happen that easily, with just one wish.

But he knew that that wasn't the case.

He lifted another prayer and watched his steps as he navigated the rocky terrain.

He wasn't sure how long it would take to get to the cave, but he estimated that it would be at least an hour until they reached the old campground area. From there, they'd have to scale the side of the cliff again.

This could end up being an all-day excursion just to get this money.

Maybe, in the meantime, Hendrix would send his men this way, despite Autumn's words last night.

Derek could wish that, at least.

Behind him, Foxglove began to whistle.

The irony of the moment wasn't lost on him. Here was a man who had the power of life and death in his hands. And he seemed so carefree, like it didn't bother him what was ruined in his path of destruction.

Men like these had made Derek decide to be a lawyer. He wanted justice for the bad guys. He needed to see them behind bars.

Ever since his mom had died during a bank robbery when he was younger, he had known he wanted to do whatever he could to stop men like this in their tracks.

As they got closer to the campsite, Derek heard the river. It sounded louder than usual. He knew what that meant— the water was even more volatile than it had been before.

A few minutes later, they reached the campsite and Derek expelled a breath.

He'd thought the banks were swollen before. But now, they were at least eight to ten feet higher than before. The sight of them took his breath away.

Autumn must have been thinking the same thing. She paused near a large boulder and shook her head as she stared at a new inlet that appeared to have formed where the campsite used to be. Water rushed from the mountainside, forming what looked like a new river.

"I didn't expect this," Autumn said.

Foxglove stopped beside her and surveyed the area. "Is this a problem?"

"In order to get to that money, we're going to have take a detour and scale the side of the rock face instead."

Foxglove pointed to the water. "Or we can cross this. We don't have time for a detour."

Autumn shook her head. "It's a bad idea. I don't know how deep it is."

Foxglove said nothing for a moment as he looked around. "There's only one way to find out."

"What are you thinking?" Autumn's voice turned hard, as if she was anticipating bad news, as if she knew his response would be something she didn't approve of.

Foxglove grabbed Derek's arm. "He'll test it out for us."

"No!" Autumn began to reach for him but dropped her hand as she saw Foxglove's warning gaze.

"I didn't ask you for your opinion," Foxglove said.

"You're asking him to die." Autumn's eyes widened with fear. "It's not safe to cross this."

"We'll never know unless we test it," Foxglove said. "If he doesn't make it across, then we'll know we need to turn around and go back."

"If he doesn't make it across, that means he's going to die." Autumn's voice cracked.

Derek stepped forward. "I'll do it."

Autumn's gaze widened even more as she looked up at him. "No, Derek. You can't…"

Derek knew what the odds were. If Autumn kept insisting that Derek couldn't do this, then they were just going to make Autumn do it. He couldn't chance that, and he knew that these guys were not going to back off.

He stared at the raging river in front of him and wondered exactly what was going to happen here. He had no idea how this would play out.

"Derek…" Autumn stared at him.

"It's okay," he told her.

Their gazes met for a moment, and he hoped he didn't have to say a word for her to know how he felt. In these few short days they'd known each other, he had developed feelings that he hadn't known were possible.

Though one part of him told himself to keep this woman at arm's length, the other part of him knew that his life was going to be forever changed after meeting her.

He didn't know what was going to happen today, but he was a better person for knowing Autumn Mercer.

She squeezed the skin between her eyes and looked away, almost as if she had resigned herself to accepting what was about to happen. Foxglove wouldn't change his mind. He'd left no doubt about that.

Foxglove pushed him forward. "Now go."

With one more look at Autumn and a pat on Sherlock's head, Derek stepped into the water.

He sucked in a breath. The water was chilly and came up to his knees.

Even though he wasn't in deep, the pull of the water was overwhelming. The rushing rapid had a strength he hadn't anticipated, like a jet stream roared beneath the surface.

"Keep moving," Foxglove said.

Derek glanced back in time to see Foxglove point the gun at Autumn.

That was what he'd thought. If didn't obey, Autumn would get hurt. He wasn't going to let that happen. Maybe—just maybe—he'd be able to make it across.

He took another step and sank to his waist.

It was definitely deeper than he had anticipated—and stronger.

Derek reached for one of the boulders that still jutted out above the surface of the water. Maybe the structure would help him keep steady.

But as he took his third step, the ground disappeared beneath his feet.

The rapids claimed him and began pulling him downstream, proving they were stronger than he was.

He heard Autumn scream.

He knew how this was going to end.

In a few minutes, Derek would go over Beaver Falls and plunge to a certain death.

NINETEEN

Autumn screamed when she saw Derek's body being swept downstream in the raging rapids. "Derek!"

She knew what this meant.

There was no way to survive what waited at the end of this river.

She started to reach forward, almost as if she might be able to grab Derek. But she knew there was no use. There was no grabbing him. The rapids were too fast, too furious. They'd pulled him away too quickly.

She wanted to close her eyes and pray, yet she couldn't seem to look away.

Derek's body was swept under the water as the river consumed him.

She held her breath, waiting to see if and when he would resurface.

Beside her, Sherlock barked, almost as if the canine had begun to care about Derek just as much as she had.

There!

Derek's head bobbed out from the water.

She released her breath, though she knew this was far from being over.

How much farther did he have until he hit the falls? Three hundred feet?

In water like this, the distance would go quickly.

Moisture pressed at her eyes as the seriousness of the situation hit her.

If only she had more time. More supplies. A team around her who might help.

She had none of those things, only a helpless feeling that pressed on her.

Dear Lord, help us!

She sucked in a breath when she saw Derek catch a fallen log.

Maybe there was hope!

But they had to somehow figure out a way to make it to him.

"Let's leave him there," Foxglove said. "We'll need to find a different way to get to the cave."

Autumn's mouth dropped open. "I'm not leaving Derek there."

He leaned closer, his rancid breath again spilling over her cheek. "You're going to do what I'm telling you to do."

She crossed her arms, a stubborn determination rising in her. It might get her killed, but she didn't even care. She couldn't live with herself if she let Derek die.

"I'm not leaving him," she said.

Foxglove raised his gun again, and she fought the urge to flinch. She braced herself for the pain she was certain would come again. Would he slap her again? Or would he just pull the trigger this time?

"You don't get to call the shots here," he finally growled.

"If you don't have me and you don't have Derek, then you can't find that money," she told him. Derek would be proud. It seemed like a good closing argument. "And that's all there is to it."

Foxglove stared at her before lowering his gaze. "You have thirty minutes. And then I don't care anymore."

She released her breath, feeling a temporary moment of relief. But she knew that would be short-lived.

Thirty minutes? It wasn't enough time. But she was going to have to see what she could do. She was certain Derek would do the same thing for her if the roles were reversed.

She glanced around her and saw that if they backtracked some and climbed over a ridge, they might be able to avoid this new section of the river that had opened up. If they could do that and get to the other side, then Autumn could walk down as close as she could to the shore and maybe reach Derek.

She was going to have to move more quickly than her body wanted to allow.

Every part of her still ached from her fall yesterday. But she could ignore that. For now.

When this was all over, she'd have plenty of time to recover and rejuvenate.

Right now, all that mattered was getting to Derek.

Sherlock seemed to understand exactly what she was doing. The dog pulled on the leash as he led her toward that ridge. The two gunmen followed behind.

Autumn hated to take her eyes off Derek, even if it was only for a few minutes. At least when she could see him, she knew he was okay, that he was still hanging on for his life.

But now that Derek was out of sight, she had no idea if he was okay. What if he couldn't hold on? What if the rapids had already pulled him from that branch and he was heading downstream again?

She shook her head. She could hardly bear the thought of that. She had to remain positive.

Autumn kept walking, kept maneuvering around the large rocks. She finally reached the area where the ground inclined. It was going to be tricky to maneuver through this area, but she felt sure that they could do it.

She watched where Sherlock stepped and then she followed behind the dog. The ground slipped beneath her, threatening her with falling into the water below.

But that didn't happen.

She didn't bother to glance behind her. Foxglove and his crony were going to have to figure out how to get through this themselves. She certainly wasn't going to offer any help. Especially since she'd been given a time limit.

"Don't get too far ahead of us," Foxglove growled.

She glanced back and saw that he was struggling to get through the tricky passage.

No doubt he wasn't normally the type of guy on the front lines of things like this. No, he was the type of guy who did backroom deals, trying to utilize every resource possible to get as much money as he could. He had men who did his dirty work for him.

The thought of it made her like this man even less, as if that were even possible.

She pressed ahead, navigating her way through the rocks, the water and the elements.

She knew not to try anything foolish. She knew if she did, those men wouldn't hesitate to pull the trigger. Then both she and Derek would be gone.

Finally, she reached the edge of the river.

Derek was still hanging on to that branch. He was still alive.

Autumn had to figure out a way to keep him like that.

Derek raised his head, trying to keep the water from rushing into his mouth.

It took all of his energy just to hang on as the water bulldozed him.

The rapids were so strong. He couldn't get over just how powerful they were.

His arms gripped the old weathered tree. If it wasn't for this downed foliage, he would be dead right now. He had no doubt about that. But he was far from being safe.

He tried to pull himself down the length of the tree back to the shore, but he couldn't. Not only was he fighting the rapids, but his shirt was stuck. He kept trying to reach back, to pull it off the broken branch that snagged it. But it was no use. He couldn't get it free.

He'd even tried to take the shirt off. But the water pressed too hard against him. It was almost impossible to move at all.

He glanced around. What was he going to do? He couldn't just stay here until he died. There had to be some other option.

He gave another tug, hoping that the fabric of his shirt would rip and release him.

It didn't.

"Derek!" he heard someone yell.

He looked up and saw Autumn scrambling down the shore toward him. His heart pounded into his chest.

She'd come for him.

But just as quickly as his hope rose, he saw Foxglove and his man following behind her. Just what were they planning now? Did he want to know?

She paused near the upended roots of the tree and stared at him, Sherlock by her side. "Can you pull yourself across the tree?"

"I'm stuck!" he yelled. "I tried, but it's no use."

Autumn frowned as she stared at him. Derek could see the wheels in her mind turning, trying to come up with a plan, a solution.

She glanced at her watch, as if time were running out.

What did that even mean? He didn't know. It didn't matter right now.

He needed to keep thinking also.

If he slipped up, he had no doubt he'd be swept into the river and over the waterfalls.

He knew he'd never survive that fall.

He had to try to get his shirt loose again. It was the only solution that made sense.

"Can you get your shirt off?" Autumn yelled.

"I've tried!" he yelled back over the roar of the water. "It's stuck. But I'll try again."

Just as he promised, he tried to work his elbow down, to get his shirt dislodged.

It didn't matter. He couldn't get it off. The water trapped him against the log and hindered his motions.

"It won't work!" Derek called.

Autumn continued to stare, her eyes studying the situation and trying to figure out a solution.

"Maybe I can climb down that log and get you free," she called.

"I can't let you do that. It's too risky."

The thought of something happening to her caused Derek's adrenaline to rush. He could not let that happen. He would rather die himself.

"It's the only solution that makes sense!" Autumn called back.

"Don't do it, Autumn. You're going to get yourself killed."

Even as he said the words, he saw Autumn walking toward him. He saw her pressing on the tree to see how stable it was against the land.

She was going to do it anyway, wasn't she?

Derek needed to think of a way to talk her out of this.

"Autumn…it's not safe. You're going to kill yourself."

"I can't just leave you there," she said. "I won't do it."

"She only has ten minutes to get you out of this or we're leaving!" Foxglove yelled.

Even from where Derek was, he could see the man gloating.

That was why Autumn was glancing at her watch. Foxglove had given her a time limit. The man truly was despicable.

"I can do this," Autumn said, creeping closer. "I can help you."

She straddled the tree and began inching her way down toward him.

"Autumn…" Derek called.

"I don't have any other choice."

"Don't do this." He had to get through to her.

"I'm not going to leave you to die."

She continued to inch toward him, but Derek could see the fear in her face. Anybody would be scared in this situation. She shouldn't be doing this.

Four feet out, the tree shifted. As it did, it pushed Derek under the water. Cold water filled his lungs.

He clawed his way back to the surface and popped his head out, coughing out the water.

Because his shirt was stuck, only his mouth and nose emerged from the water.

Every time a rapid swelled, liquid filled his mouth again.

Derek knew with certainty that he was not going to survive this.

The last thing Derek heard was Autumn yelling his name.

This was her fault, Autumn realized. She'd put weight on the tree, which shifted it. She couldn't continue to creep out unless she wanted to drown him.

Now Derek was stuck under the water, and she didn't know how to fix it.

If she got into the water, too, she knew there was a good chance that she would be swept away with the rapids.

Then she would be no good to Derek.

But she meant it when she said she wasn't going to leave him here.

"Five minutes," Foxglove called behind her.

The man was heartless. She wanted nothing more than to put this man in his place. But this wasn't the time, nor did she have the resources or the leverage to do so.

Right now, all she could do was focus on helping Derek.

She glanced around. There had to be something else she could do.

But she had no idea what.

But she couldn't give up hope.

Almost as if Sherlock read her mind, the dog scrambled down the tree past her. She'd let go of the leash and left him on the shore.

But she had never expected the canine to follow her.

Panic surged through her.

What was the dog doing?

"Sherlock!" she called.

She looked farther downstream at the river. Looked at the rapids there. Imagined her dog getting swept away in them.

Her heart pounded with premature grief.

She could not lose her dog, too.

"Sherlock!" she called again.

But the dog kept walking down the tree, his balance perfect.

What was he doing?

Autumn kept her eyes open and began to pray fervently for his protection. For Derek's protection.

Everything felt out of control right now. Out of her hands. And she didn't know how to fix it.

She liked fixing things. She liked being in control.

But there was nothing about this situation right now that made her feel like she could do anything. She was helpless.

As Sherlock dived into the water, she felt a tear trickle down her cheek. "Sherlock! No!"

Her body sank into the tree as her dog disappeared under the rapids. This was not the way that things were supposed to turn out. She'd been praying so hard for a happy ending.

"You might as well come back to us now," Foxglove called. "It's over."

Could his words be true? Was this all over? Autumn didn't want to believe it.

Her gaze fastened on the scene. Sherlock had gone under the water. What was he doing? Had he already been carried farther downstream?

Seconds ticked passed.

A moment later, her dog's head bobbed to the surface. There was something in his mouth.

Was that…fabric?

The dog went back under water one more time, and Autumn held her breath, watching and waiting to see what he was doing.

The next moment, he reemerged, nudging something with him.

Was that… Derek?

He was barely lucid, but he was free from the branch he'd been stuck on.

Sherlock must have chewed through his shirt and set him loose.

Her heart let out a triumphant cry.

But she knew without a doubt that things were far from being over.

Derek clung to the tree with one arm and Sherlock with the other. He looked like he was barely hanging on.

But the good news was that he *was* hanging on.

Now that he was above the water, Autumn could creep farther down the tree. She began to scoot down the log with both of her legs wrapped around the trunk.

When she got close enough, she grabbed Sherlock from the water. She pulled him onto the log and kissed his wet head. "Good boy…"

She lifted the dog until he was behind her, walking back to toward the shore. Then she turned back to Derek.

How could she leverage his body? She was going to need his help.

She reached forward and grabbed his arm. "You can do this."

He said nothing, but she could see that determination in his gaze. He was far from giving up.

He pulled himself down the tree. Autumn moved slowly with him. She wasn't going to let go of him. She needed to be like his safety harness in case anything went wrong.

Finally, Derek's feet must have hit the bottom. He crawled back to dry land and collapsed there.

But the important thing was that he was okay.

For now.

TWENTY

Derek lay against the ground and let out a cough.

Against all the odds, he had survived. He was on dry land.

And it was all thanks to Sherlock and Autumn. Those two were truly lifesavers.

He had been certain when he went underwater that last time that he was never going to come back up.

Then he'd felt the claws against his back. He'd known that Sherlock had come to rescue him.

He owed both Sherlock and Autumn his life. He just hoped that he had a chance to thank them one day.

Someone kicked his side, and he let out a moan.

"Get up. We're wasting time." Foxglove glared down at him from above.

Derek pushed himself to his feet. As he did, Autumn's worried face came into view. She touched his arm, silently asking him if he was okay.

"We need to keep moving," Foxglove ordered. "We've already wasted too much time."

"He almost died," Autumn barked. "Give him a moment."

"We don't have a minute. You're lucky I gave you as much time as I did."

Autumn glared at Foxglove and kept an arm on Derek. "You okay?"

He ran a hand through his hair and nodded. "I am. Thank you both."

"I hate to break up this reunion, but move." Foxglove shoved Derek, pushing them downstream.

"You need to back off." Autumn's voice rose with defiance. "We're not going to be any good to you if we're dead."

Foxglove only offered a cold stare. "Don't make me repeat myself. Now, where do we need to go from here?"

Autumn glanced around before her gaze stopped at a cliff in the distance. "Up there."

"And how do you propose we get up there?"

"We're going to have to climb. I hope you're ready for it."

Derek dreaded it. His body felt weak. Spent.

But he would do whatever he had to do to keep Autumn and Sherlock safe, as well as his brother. He'd use every last bit of his strength if he had to.

"Move!" Foxglove said.

With one last worried glance at him, Autumn grabbed Sherlock's leash and started toward the cliff in the distance.

Derek followed behind, still coughing up water. The air was cold in his lungs, promising certain sickness.

Nothing about this situation was good.

Nothing.

They trudged down the shoreline, dodging fallen trees and debris that had been pushed over by the water.

Finally, they reached the area where the ground began to climb.

"We'll need to watch our steps in here," Autumn said.

She didn't wait for Foxglove to acknowledge what she said. Instead, she and Sherlock began to scale the side of the mountain. A few minutes later, they were walking on the same ledge they'd traveled a couple days ago.

As he moved carefully, Derek still couldn't stop thinking about how William could have done this to him. If his brother had just made wise choices, they'd never be in this mess.

But Derek supposed it was too late to look back. All he could do right now was look forward and try to fix the wrongs that had already been done.

And right now, he had a bigger challenge ahead of him.

His head was still spinning from that near-death experience. His shoes were wet. His muscles felt strained.

Navigating this ledge wasn't easy on a good day. But right now, it could be even more deadly. He had to pour all his attention into each step.

Autumn glanced back and felt worry pulse through her.

Derek was in no state to navigate this right now. But she knew that Foxglove wouldn't care. The man was determined to get his money, no matter whose life it cost.

The best thing Autumn could do right now was to try to keep a calm disposition and a clear head.

That's what Kevin had always told her.

What would he say if he knew what was going on right now?

He'd want her to be smart.

He would also give his blessing for falling in love.

Her back straightened at the thought.

Where had that come from? It was so out of the blue. Right now, all she should be thinking about was survival.

But somehow the thought that Kevin would approve of a new relationship crossed her mind.

It didn't make sense.

But Autumn did know that when she'd seen Derek out there, his life on the line…that she'd feared losing him, feared letting him go.

Once this was over, maybe they could talk about what was going on between the two of them. Maybe she could make sense of all these emotions she was thinking and feeling.

They continued down the ledge. She was almost to the area where they would need to turn the narrow corner and then navigate into the cove where the cave was located.

The water was considerably higher this time, even more than she'd seen in all her years working for the park. On the other hand, it didn't surprise her.

The storm system had hovered over them for nearly three days, just dumping water on them. As the bigger rivers overflowed, they emptied out in the smaller rivers like this one.

It was no wonder that Hendrix had his hands full right now. She had seen firsthand all the damage that storm had been capable of.

"You doing okay?" she asked Derek quietly. She glanced back to see his expression.

He looked paler than she would like to see, but he nodded. "I'm fine. Thank you."

But his voice sounded weak. His motions looked like they took entirely too much effort.

She had to think of a plan to get them out of this. It was all there was to it.

Just then an idea fluttered into her mind.

Would it work?

She wasn't sure. But it was at least worth a try.

But she was going to have to be very careful if she wanted to enact her plan without any casualties.

* * *

Derek sucked in a breath as he heard commotion behind him.

He glanced behind him in time to see Foxglove's foot slip.

Before he slid down the mountain, Montgomery grabbed his arm and pulled him back up.

But Derek saw the flash of fear on the man's face.

He'd thought he was going to die.

Derek understood the sentiment. His life had flashed before his eyes, too.

Part of him wondered what these men would do once they had that money they were after. Would they shoot him and Autumn and leave them in the cave?

He wouldn't put it past them.

Though one part of Derek wanted to be the hero and try to take these guys out, the other part of him knew that would be foolish. It could end up with them all dead. Besides, he didn't have a weapon.

For that reason, Derek thought the best move might be just to be compliant and to be on guard.

He just hoped that assumption paid off.

Just ahead, he spotted the entrance to the cave. Not much farther, and they would be there. They continued to walk, watching their steps, even as weariness pressed into them.

Finally, they reached the entrance.

Autumn moved aside the sapling that blocked the cave's mouth and nodded inside. "The backpack is in here."

"Ladies first," Foxglove said.

Autumn's eyes narrowed with irritation, but she slipped inside. Derek followed behind her, memories flashing back to him. Memories of sitting around the fire inside and talking to Autumn, getting to know her better. Memories of listening to the rain and thunder outside from the cave's entrance, pretending for a moment that everything was normal. Memories of seeing that bobcat outside.

Was it possible that had just happened a couple days ago? The events of this week seemed so surreal.

Foxglove and his man climbed in beside them, and they all huddled near the old fire pit where he and Autumn had kept warm.

But something was wrong.

Autumn and Derek glanced at each other.

The book bag was gone.

"Where is it?" Foxglove growled.

"It was here when we left." Autumn pointed to the ground. "Right, Derek?"

"She's telling the truth. It was there."

"Then what could've happened to it? Because I have a feeling you two are lying to me." Foxglove raised his gun and pointed it at Autumn again. "You led me out here for nothing."

Derek felt the anger growing inside him. He could not let that man hurt Autumn. They'd been through too much.

"Somebody better start talking or I'm going to start shooting," Foxglove said.

"Why don't you put down that gun so we can have a rational conversation?" Derek raised his hands as he tried to talk some sense into the man.

"I'm the one making those decisions," Foxglove said. "Now where is it?"

"I don't know," Autumn said. "I'm telling the truth. It was right here."

Foxglove raised the gun and pulled the trigger.

As he did, Derek dived toward him.

But it didn't matter.

A rumble sounded around him.

Were they facing another rockslide?

And what did that mean if they were inside this cave?

TWENTY-ONE

Autumn heard the roar.

The sound of that bullet must have set off a rockslide.

The last thing they needed was to get trapped inside this cave, especially with Foxglove.

As the rumbles continued, they knocked Autumn off her feet. She hit the slick ground in the cave. She clung to it for a minute, trying to gain her balance.

"We need to get out of here!" she yelled.

Derek grabbed her and helped her to her feet as everyone scrambled toward the entrance.

But was it too late?

She heard the rocks falling down the cliff face just outside the cave.

They emerged and scooted down the ledge just as the rocks tumbled over the cave's entrance. A few smaller rocks skipped and bounced, pummeling their arms and legs.

But the large rocks appeared contained several feet away.

If they hadn't gotten out when they did, they would have all been stuck in there.

Autumn could count her blessings that hadn't happened. Just as the thought entered her mind, a stray rock plummeted down the cliff. She glanced up just in time to see it hit Foxglove's man.

He tumbled into the basin below, yelling as he fell to his certain death.

"Montgomery!" Foxglove yelled, staring down at his friend.

Derek grabbed Autumn, and his body covered hers as more stray rocks rained down from above.

He was willing to take the brunt of this.

Warmth spread through her. Warmth and concern.

She didn't want anything to happen to him because of her. At the same time, she felt powerless to stop it.

Instead, she stood there, trying to catch her breath. Trying to wait for the next wave of rocks. Trying not to panic.

Finally, the rumbles stopped.

After a couple seconds of silence, they all turned and looked at each other.

Autumn's gaze went to Foxglove's hands.

Somehow, he'd managed to grab his gun in the midst of all that.

She followed his gaze as he looked down into the basin below.

His friend lay there, his body a crumpled mess.

There was no way he'd survived that.

Foxglove turned toward her, anger heating his gaze. "This is your fault!"

"This is because you pulled that trigger," Autumn said. "Don't put this on us."

"Montgomery is dead because of you." He raised his gun again and aimed it at her.

"You do know if you pull that trigger again, then we're all dead," Derek reminded him.

Foxglove remained quiet for a moment. Finally, realization seemed to roll over his features. He snarled as he lowered his weapon. "Where's the money?"

"It's like we said, we don't know," Autumn said. "I don't know what it's going to take for you to believe us."

"Who else knew about this cave?" he demanded.

"Nobody but us…" Her voice trailed off.

"And who?"

Autumn glanced at Derek. "Us and that bobcat."

He snorted. "You're saying a bobcat stole my money?"

"She's saying the bobcat could've come back for food and carried that backpack away from here in the process," Derek finished.

As Derek said those words, Autumn glanced below her. If that cat had come back and gotten the backpack, he probably wouldn't have carried the whole thing back with him to his den.

As if to confirm that thought, she saw a swath of khaki down below.

It was the same color as the backpack.

But she dared not speak the words aloud.

She didn't have to.

Foxglove followed her gaze and spotted the bag. "That's it, isn't it?"

Autumn didn't say anything.

"You need to go get it," Foxglove said.

Derek shook his head. "If we go down there, it's going to be another death wish."

"I don't care. I want to know if my money is in there."

Autumn felt the familiar tension thread through her muscles again. She knew there was no way to talk this man out of it. She also knew that Derek was in no shape to climb down there himself. She was their best bet.

But this wouldn't be an easy feat. She didn't have the right gear or the right shoes to do it.

However, she wouldn't be able to convince Foxglove of that.

Derek felt apprehension ripple through him as worst-case scenarios played out in his mind. Autumn would be risking her life if she did this.

He grabbed her arm. "Don't do it."

"I don't have any other choice," she said, her voice sounding strained but stubborn.

"She's right," Foxglove said. "I'm getting that money one way or another."

Derek squared up against him. "People's lives are more important than money."

Foxglove let out a deep chuckle. "Maybe to you. Not me. Now, I really don't need both of you around. So you can either decide which one of you is going to get that backpack, or you can decide which one of you wants to die first."

Derek glanced at Autumn. He knew without a doubt that this man was telling the truth. He wouldn't hesitate to kill them.

Autumn stepped toward him. "I'll do it."

"Autumn…" Derek's voice trailed off.

"I can do this." Her gaze implored him. "I am our best bet."

He knew it was true. "But…"

She touched his arm. "I'll be okay. But I'm going to need your belt."

"My belt?"

"That's right. It can act as a safety line for me. At least until I can get to this next ledge."

He nodded, not questioning her. "Whatever you need."

With hesitation in her gaze, she glanced at Foxglove one last time, casting him a dirty look. Then she climbed down on her knees and began to lower herself down the rocks. She worked slowly, finding the right footholds to assure she wouldn't slip.

Derek watched, holding his breath and praying she'd be okay. Just as he did the first time they'd had to grab this backpack, he lowered himself onto the ground. Sherlock remained beside him, acting as a sidekick in case he needed something.

Derek released his breath when he saw Autumn make it to the first ledge below. Just one more, and she should be able to reach that backpack.

Now that Derek looked at it more closely, it became clear that that bobcat had come back. He saw the teeth marks and saw how the fabric had been torn apart. There had been some sealed food inside, but the cat must have smelled it.

He glanced around quickly, making sure that the creature wasn't lingering anywhere close.

He saw nothing.

Autumn continued to climb downward. He knew the woman well enough to know she was careful and well thought out. That realization brought him comfort now.

Foxglove, on the other hand, tapped his foot beside him, obviously impatient with how slowly things were moving. He was going to have to wait. There was no other way to get around the situation. But Derek had a feeling the man wouldn't care about that.

Finally, Autumn reached the bottom. She lifted the backpack up and showed Foxglove. "Got it."

"Make sure the money is inside," he said.

Derek prayed that the money was there. If it wasn't, he didn't know how the rest of the day was going to play out.

She opened and riffled through it. A moment later, she pulled out a bag of cash. "Happy now?"

"Throw it to me," he said.

Derek's stomach clenched. What exactly what was the

man thinking right now? His gut feeling told him it probably wasn't anything good. Derek and Autumn were just a means to an end, as far as this man was concerned.

"Can't I just carry it back up?" Autumn asked.

"You need both of your hands to climb back up. You know that. Throw it to me."

After moment of hesitation, Autumn did just that.

Foxglove got it and examined the bag for a moment before a satisfied smile crossed his face.

"Good job." He then pointed his gun down at Autumn. "Now, you've outlived your usefulness, and I need to get rid of the dead weight."

"No!" Derek yelled.

It couldn't end this way—and he would give his life to assure that it didn't.

Autumn held her breath when she saw Foxglove had pulled the gun again. He was going to kill her, wasn't he?

But before he could pull the trigger, Derek's leg swept out and hit the man behind the ankles.

Foxglove fell to the ground, his gun clattering on the ledge below.

She continued to watch, hardly able to breathe as Derek and Foxglove began to wrestle.

Derek threw a punch, hitting Foxglove in the face. Foxglove came right back and punched him in the gut.

Both of them were on the ledge, and at any minute, either of them could slip. Or their actions could set off another rock slide.

Dear Lord, help us now.

They struggled to see who could reach the gun first. Her stomach sank when she saw Foxglove grab it. He aimed it at Derek, who raised his hands.

"I should kill you now," Foxglove grumbled.

Derek said nothing. No doubt, he knew there was no changing his mind.

Dread surged through Autumn as she waited to see what would happen.

Foxglove raised his chin, something changing in his eyes. He lowered his gun—but only slightly.

"But I won't," he said. "I like you. You're a fighter. Not like your brother."

Autumn released the air from her lungs and rubbed Sherlock's head.

"You guys could be useful, so I'll give you one more chance," Foxglove muttered. "Don't blow it."

She knew better than to trust a criminal. But maybe they had just bought a little time.

She glanced up at Derek and saw blood trickling from the side of his mouth.

But he was alive. She was thankful for that at least.

"I'm coming up," she said.

Derek looked down at her, climbing on his stomach again so he could assist her.

Autumn knew coming back up was going to be harder than going down. Momentum wouldn't be working in her favor. Plus, her muscles felt tired, spent.

She made it back to the second ledge. But this would be the hardest part here.

Derek lowered the belt down to her, and she grabbed onto it like a lifeline.

"I got you," he said. "I won't let go."

And somehow, Autumn knew that he wouldn't. She trusted him.

She grabbed the belt with one hand and began her ascent with the other.

Derek helped her and pulled at the belt, raising her upward. As soon as her arms reached the ledge, he grabbed her and pulled her up beside him.

She was safe.

For now.

Sherlock came and licked her face.

"I'm glad to see you, too, boy." She rubbed his head.

"Enough!" Foxglove said. "We've got to get back to the camp. I have more that needs to be done. So can we wrap all of this up?"

Autumn and Derek exchanged a glance. Just what was he planning now?

She almost didn't want to know.

TWENTY-TWO

Derek felt the weariness pressing in on him as he walked down the ledge again. With any luck, this would be the last time he would need to do this…forever.

The good news was now they were down to Derek, Autumn and Sherlock against Foxglove. However, Foxglove had a gun, and they didn't.

Derek had expected to see more remorse and mourning from the man after he'd lost his friend. But there had been nothing. That just drove home the point that this man was dangerous and heartless.

Derek's gaze hit Autumn as she walked in front of him, her hand on Sherlock's leash. The dog was a natural out here, not uncomfortable in the least as he scaled this mountainside. Derek was so glad that Autumn and Sherlock were okay. If only he could promise them that they would be okay into the future. But he knew that wasn't a promise that he could make.

Finally, they reached the end of the ledge. Carefully, they climbed around the water that had almost killed Derek earlier.

He shuddered as he remembered those moments. He'd come close to losing his life. Having that happen had confirmed one thing to him.

Life was too short not to take risks.

Though part of him had wanted to keep people at arm's length ever since his father had died and Sarah had left him at the altar, that was no way to live. No one knew how much time they had left on this earth, and they had to make the best of what we did have.

As soon as Derek got out of the situation—and that was the way he was going to continue thinking about this—he was going to make some changes in his life.

And they *were* going to get out of this. Derek was going to focus on the positive here. This man was not smarter than they were. If it wasn't for the man's gun, he had no doubt that they could take him.

He tried to think through what might happen once they got back to the camp. Obviously, William owed this man more than ten thousand. And Derek knew without a doubt that Foxglove was not going to walk away with any less than that.

It was like he'd said earlier—his reputation was on the line here. If other people that Foxglove worked with saw him as weak, they would walk all over him.

Derek had seen enough drug lords in action to know how these types of people operated. Foxglove was cut from the same cloth as some of those men Derek had put behind bars. He was all about money and power, no matter the cost.

Ahead of him, he saw Autumn was beginning to limp. Her body had been through so much, and she was clearly in pain. He wished more than anything that he could help her.

He crept forward and touched her arm. "Are you okay?"

"It's just my leg from where I hit it yesterday. It's sore, but I'll be okay."

"You don't look okay." He examined her face and saw

how pale it was. She was in pain. Scaling the side of that mountain must have only made her injuries worse for her.

"Let me tell Foxglove if we need to stop," Derek said.

She shook her head. "We can't do that. You know he won't care."

"What are you two whispering about up there?" Foxglove asked.

"She's hurt." Derek turned toward him.

"Yeah? So what? My friend's dead. You think I'm going to feel sorry for you?"

Derek felt the anger burning inside him. "Autumn helped to get your money. She didn't have to do that."

"That might mean more if I hadn't had a gun to her head when she did it. It wasn't exactly out of the kindness of her heart." He let out a rough chuckle.

Just then, Autumn moaned, and her eyes implored Foxglove's. "Can we stop? Just for a minute? Please."

Foxglove grunted. Finally, he nodded. "Just a minute then. We don't have time to waste."

Autumn leaned against one of the rocks and closed her eyes, leaning into her good leg and stretching out her other one.

She needed to see a doctor.

So did Derek's brother.

This wilderness was not the place where anyone wanted to get hurt, especially in these conditions.

She let go of Sherlock's leash and leaned down toward the dog, whispering something in his ear. It was obvious how much comfort she found in the canine, and right now it was no different.

Then she leaned back and closed her eyes, almost as if absorbing the sun and hoping it would reinvigorate her.

Derek glanced behind him and saw Foxglove standing there, his gun still in hand, finger still close enough to the trigger to use it if he needed to. As his gaze swerved back toward Autumn, he saw her eyes widen as she looked at something in the distance.

"Sherlock," she murmured, her voice listless.

Foxglove straightened, following the dog with his gaze. "Where is he going?"

"I can run and get him." Derek stepped that way.

"No." She grabbed his arm. "It's too late. He must have seen a squirrel and run off."

Derek narrowed his eyes. In all the time that he had been around Sherlock, he'd never seen the dog do that.

He stared at Autumn for a moment. What wasn't she telling him?

Autumn's heart pounded in her ears. She hoped she made the right choice. She had told Sherlock to go.

She'd whispered in his ear, "Home!"

She knew those words would send him back to the parking lot. She knew the dog was smart enough to get there. Her only hope was that the rangers would be there when he arrived and that the dog could lead them back to Autumn.

She had been quietly sending SOS signals from her radio all morning. Then she had turned it off, just in case someone tried to reply to her.

It was her last-ditch effort to get them out of here. But she was out of ideas as to what else to do.

Her leg hurt but not as much as she let on. She mostly wanted to stop to give Sherlock an excuse to go running ahead. But, as she looked at Derek's eyes, she saw the confusion there. She hoped to be able to explain all of this to him. Soon.

"Who cares about that stupid dog anyway?" Foxglove asked. "Let's get moving. One less mouth to feed, right?"

Autumn stood, making sure her face was etched with

pain. She wanted to take her time getting back to the camp. That would give Sherlock time to get to the parking lot and for backup to arrive.

She had a feeling that once they got back to the camp, Foxglove had another plan for getting more money. It was the only thing that made sense. If she was in this man's shoes, then she would want to get out of this wilderness as soon as she could so she could arrange some type of way to get the cash that was rightfully hers.

Foxglove shoved Derek forward.

Derek looked back, his eyes narrowed with indignation. But he kept himself calm and in control.

She could appreciate that.

So many people would have lashed out by now. But lashing out could get him killed. It could get them both killed. So she counted her blessings that he wasn't that type.

Yet Derek was still strong. There was a lot of strength to be found in self-control and in being quiet. She admired that.

She looked ahead. They probably had another forty minutes until they reached the campsite. She prayed for whatever would happen once they got there. And she prayed for William and his injury.

And, of course, she prayed that their plan worked.

Derek was still trying to figure out what had happened between Autumn and Sherlock. Her gaze told him there was more to the story. Had she let the dog go on purpose? Why would she do that? Wasn't it more dangerous for the dog out in the wild than it would be with them?

He didn't know, but he was going to have to put his faith in Autumn right now.

As he got closer to the campsite, the tension in his stomach pulled tighter. He didn't know what was going to happen next or what condition his brother was in. He hated to think about his brother being in pain. Even though William, in some ways, had done this to himself, he still hated to see this.

He had a broken his leg, but William had also been shot in the arm. How was Foxglove expecting him to get out of this wilderness?

Even if they were planning on taking William to a bank or some type of financial institution so he could transfer money, how were they going to justify his appearance when they were there?

It didn't make sense.

William needed to be in one piece. Otherwise, the people working at the bank would have to realize that he was under duress. Not only did he look horrible, but the wound in his shoulder and his broken leg would be a dead giveaway.

Derek's stomach felt even more unsettled than before.

Something was wrong here. What were they missing?

Finally, the camp came into view.

Whitaker ran back toward them. Questions laced his gaze.

"Montgomery didn't make it," Foxglove said.

Derek watched as the man's face fell. This man wasn't as heartless as Foxglove. He actually cared that his friend had died.

"You couldn't help him?" Whitaker asked.

"It was too late," Foxglove said. "He hit the rocks too hard. Ask them. They saw the same."

The man looked at Autumn, and she nodded. "I'm sorry. He slipped."

The man stepped closer to her, his muscles bristling with anger. "Did you do this?"

"She didn't have anything to do with it," Derek said. "Leave her alone."

"You don't get a say-so here," the man said, leaving Autumn and going to leer at Derek instead.

That's what Derek had intended—to take the attention off Autumn.

"I'm just telling you what happened," Derek said, keeping his head up high.

"We don't have time for this," Foxglove said. "We have things we need to get done."

He pointed his gun at Autumn and Derek, indicating for them to go farther into the camp.

Derek searched his surroundings, looking for his brother.

He didn't see him. He waited until he reached the tents to ask any questions. But his brother clearly wasn't tied up to the tree as he had been earlier.

"Where's William?" he asked.

"He's in his tent," Whitaker said before spitting on the ground in disgust.

"Why?" Derek asked.

"Because he was whining too much. Crying about how much it hurt. I got tired of listening to it." The man's nostrils flared.

"What do you plan on doing now?" Derek asked.

"Beats me."

"William…" Derek muttered.

He stepped toward the tent. Nobody stopped him.

Quickly, he unzipped it and peered inside.

His brother lay on a sleeping bag there, unmoving.

"William?" Derek rushed toward him and knelt beside him.

But his brother didn't respond.

Concern rushed through Derek as he reached to check his pulse.

He prayed his brother was still alive.

But he had a bad feeling about this.

TWENTY-THREE

Autumn saw the concern on Derek's face as he rushed inside his brother's tent.

Her heart sank as she waited.

Was William dead?

Her pulse pounded in her ears as she waited to hear what Derek had discovered. She wished she could rush to him, that she could help him. But with that gun on her, she knew she shouldn't make any moves.

Derek stood from the tent and glared at Foxglove. "He's still alive, but barely. He's not even conscious. He needs help."

"Sorry." Foxglove shrugged, apathy obvious in his lifeless gaze. "But he should've thought about that before he got himself into this mess."

"You…" Derek growled, his fists clenched at his side.

Autumn sensed that Derek was about to do something he would regret. She could tell by looking at his eyes and reading his body language that he was ready to charge at the man and tackle him to the ground.

Before he could do that, her arm shot out to stop him.

"He's not worth it," she said. "Fighting him right now won't do any good. It's just going to get you killed, too."

She watched as Derek's intense gaze finally softened.

He closed his eyes and looked away, as if reality was finally sinking in.

"You're right," he muttered.

"We've got to get out of here," Foxglove said. "We have some ATVs stashed about an hour west of here. We can get there, then I can get one of my guys to pick us up."

"ATVs?" Autumn asked. "How many of them do you have?"

It probably didn't matter. Because there were only two of these men, and they had three hostages.

That meant that this man had no intentions of leaving with all three of them.

The thought did not make her feel any better.

"We can't leave William here." Derek put his hands on his hips, standing his ground as they stood there at the camp.

"You can come back later and get him." Foxglove brushed him off as he took a step toward the woods.

"He's not going to make it that long."

"Do you want to carry him through this wilderness?" Foxglove stared at Derek, waiting for his response.

Derek knew that wasn't a possibility. His brother was too injured, too heavy. There was no way to navigate these woods with his brother over his shoulders. If he could do it, he would.

"I can stay here with him." Autumn's gaze met his.

Derek knew she was trying to say something. He didn't know what, though. Did she know something that he didn't?

"We're not leaving you here," Foxglove said. "All of us are going. Now. No questions asked."

Derek felt the anger continue to rise in him. "How can you just leave William to die?"

"That's just the nature of this business. He should've known better than to get involved with me."

Derek still didn't move. "How are you going to get his money if he's dead?"

A subtle smile lit Foxglove's face. "I have my ways."

Derek tried to think like this man was, and he could only come to one conclusion—and it wasn't a possibility he wanted to face. But it was the only thing that made sense.

"I'm never going to pass as William, if that's what you're thinking. We've lost touch over the years. I don't know his passcode or PIN numbers. I definitely don't have his fingerprints."

"No, but you have other things that we could use."

Derek shook his head, still trying to figure out what he was thinking. "What does that mean?"

"You'll see soon enough."

He crossed his arms. "No, you want me to live, and it's for a reason. What is that?"

"I said you'll see." Foxglove stepped closer, hatred obvious in his gaze.

Derek's mind continued to race, trying to put things in place. The answers were right there on the edge of his consciousness. He just had to connect them.

"This isn't about William's money at all, is it?" Realization washed through him.

Foxglove didn't say anything, he just waited for him to continue.

"You want my money," Derek muttered.

"Your brother is broke," Foxglove said. "He doesn't have anything to give us. But he told us that you did."

Derek felt his eyes widened. "William wouldn't tell you that."

"But he did. Why do you think we went back to the

campsite to find you? It was because we knew if we wanted that money, then we needed to find you."

Things began to click into place in Derek's mind. Now it made sense why these men kept following them. It wasn't to use them as leverage. It was his money.

Derek had saved up a nice nest egg as an attorney. He wasn't one to go out on spending sprees or to take lavish vacations. But he did have a decent savings account in his name.

"I'm not giving you my money." Derek narrowed his gaze.

Foxglove raised his gun and pointed it at Autumn. "I'm sure we can think of ways to make it happen."

"This whole time out here…was it about William or was it about me?"

"Your brother is the one who started all of this. He really did take a loan from us, and he really cannot pay it back. When we found him out here, we knew we needed to think of ways for him to be creative and get that cash. In one of his moments of agony, he said your name. So here we are now."

"Unbelievable…"

"He also said in his moment of delirium that he brought your savings account routing number."

Derek sucked in a breath. That's what those numbers had been in his backpack. His brother had planned on taking money from his account.

Derek stared at Foxglove as he processed everything. "You're despicable, to say the least."

"Maybe we are. But we're rich. And that's how we want to keep it."

Derek saw the determination in Foxglove's gaze. These guys were planning to keep Autumn hostage until they got the money they wanted. But, if Derek had to guess, they wouldn't keep her alive after they got their hands on this money.

Derek couldn't bear the thought of losing her now.

He had to think of a way to put an end to this.

Now.

As Autumn stood in the middle of the campsite, she listened to the conversation, feeling her jaw drop with every new revelation.

These men had been after Derek this whole time. Everything started to make sense.

She didn't want to think that William would have sold out his brother, but people did strange things when they were in pain. Kind of like an animal who'd been injured. You just never knew how they were going to act out, even to those they loved.

She also knew that this situation would not have a good outcome. No matter which way she looked at it, there was no way these guys were going to let her and Derek walk away.

No, they were both going to be goners.

Not to mention William. Leaving him behind here would be signing his death certificate.

Her thoughts went back to Sherlock. The canine should have gotten back to the parking lot by now. The question was, were the other rangers there waiting for him?

It was a question she couldn't answer. She hoped Hendrix got her SOS. She hoped they could read between the lines and knew Sherlock would be able to lead them back here. She also hoped that the roads were passable.

But still there were a lot of unknowns in that situation.

Most of all, right now she hoped that Sherlock was okay. Letting him go was a bit risky. The more she thought about it, the more doubts crept into her mind.

What if her dog encountered a wild animal? Or got lost?

No, those thoughts were ridiculous. Sherlock was smarter than that.

But stress snowballed inside her.

"We need to move," Foxglove said. "Now."

He took Autumn's arm and began leading her way.

As he did, Autumn glanced back. If they left with these men, she felt certain they would die.

The question was, how were they going to get out of this?

They needed a distraction.

Almost as if Derek had read her mind, he froze and pointed at something in the distance. "The bobcat! He came back!"

As the man looked away, Derek burst into action. He grabbed Foxglove's gun from him, ready to fight for his life.

Foxglove turned and swung his arm, connecting it with Derek's face. As he did, the gun flew to the ground.

Derek reeled back.

As he did, the other man came at him.

Autumn lunged to the ground, trying to reach the gun.

Just as her hands gripped the metal there, Foxglove's foot came down over her fingers and the barrel.

Pain squeezed her.

As she looked up, she saw murder in the man's eyes.

TWENTY-FOUR

"No!" Derek yelled.

If Foxglove got that gun back, Autumn was a goner. So was he.

He dived toward the man. Before he could reach him, Whitaker appeared and tackled him.

Derek kicked the man's legs. Whitaker rolled off him, just in time for Derek to swing his leg out and hit Foxglove's knee.

The man lost his balance and fell to the ground.

As he did, Autumn reached forward, her face straining as she grabbed the gun and sat up. "Stay right where you are!"

Foxglove started to reach for her. When he saw her point the gun at him, he froze.

"Nobody move," Autumn repeated, her voice just above a growl as she pushed herself to her feet.

Foxglove stared at her, his eyes looking dazed. Finally, he raised his hands in the air also. "Let's not be hasty."

"One wrong move, and I won't hesitate to pull this trigger," Autumn continued.

"What are you going to do?" Foxglove muttered. "Are you going to arrest us? While we're stuck out here in the middle of nowhere?"

The man was taunting her. But Autumn didn't look a bit flustered as she stared the man down.

"You're going to do exactly what I tell you to do." She kept her gun pointed at them and her voice hard. "Derek, tie them up," she said. "We need to make sure they're not going anywhere."

"You don't want to do this," Foxglove said, warning snaking through his voice.

"Don't tell me what I want to do."

"This isn't going to work out the way that you think it is," Foxglove continued, undeterred by her hardened voice. The man looked like he could strike again at any moment.

"I don't need you telling me what I'm going to do or what I'm going to think," Autumn said, her voice unwavering. "Do you understand?"

Derek grabbed some rope and tied Foxglove's hands behind him, working quickly before they could try anything.

"You don't have a plan right now," Foxglove continued to mock her. "If you leave me out here, we're just going to figure out a way to get away. You know we will."

Autumn raised the gun in the air and pulled the trigger.

The gunfire cracked the air, and birds in the trees above scattered at the sound, squawking their displeasure.

"Enough talking," she said. "Do I make myself clear?"

Foxglove quieted.

Derek continued to tie up the men. Just as he pulled the last knot, a new sound filled the air.

"Is that… ?" He straightened and glanced in the distance.

It was.

It was the sound of an engine.

And it was coming their way.

He continued staring through the woods just in time to see an ATV emerge.

Was it more bad guys coming to attack them? Did Fox-glove have a backup out there?

He glanced at Autumn, trying to read her expression. She still looked composed and unflappable as she held her gun, waiting for someone to make a wrong move.

More noise filled the air.

More ATVs.

Derek really hoped it was the good guys on their way. Because if this was more bad guys, then he and Autumn were in serious trouble.

As the vehicles stopped nearby, he saw several park rangers darting through the wilderness toward them.

Help was here. Praise God, help was here.

Autumn had never been so glad to see Ranger Hendrix arrive. As the crew took over the scene, she lowered her gun and released her breath.

Maybe this was finally over.

It almost seemed too good to be true.

She watched in the distance as Derek ran into his broth-er's tent. He emerged a moment later. "He's still alive!"

Two park rangers hurried inside to help. Derek hesi-tatingly left. There probably wasn't much room to work in there.

A moment later, he appeared beside her. As soon as Autumn saw him, she threw her arms around him, nearly collapsing in his embrace.

"Good job back there," he murmured. "You saved our lives."

"I'm so glad you're okay," she whispered in his ear, pulling him tighter.

She took a step back but reached up and rested her hand on his cheek. She'd have more time to talk to him later. There was so much she wanted to say. Needed to say.

But this wasn't the time or the place.

Instead, Autumn glanced around. Her gaze searched the wilderness, and she held her breath with expectation. A moment later, she spotted another ranger cutting through the forest.

There, on a leash in front of the ranger, was... Sherlock.

The ranger released the dog, and Autumn knelt down onto the ground with her arms open. Her dog ran right into them and began licking her face.

"I knew you wouldn't let me down, Sherlock. I knew it." She held her dog closer, grateful that he was okay.

"That was some quick thinking on your part." Ranger Hendrix paced to a stop beside her.

"So you got my messages?" Autumn asked, standing to talk.

"We heard you sending the SOS through the radio. We tried to get back in touch with you but couldn't. I put everything together and realized that you were in trouble. When I saw Sherlock, I knew we didn't have any time to waste. We had to find you."

"I'm so glad you did."

"Now that we know your coordinates, we're sending a helicopter," Hendrix said, turning toward Derek. "We'll get your brother the help he needs."

"Thank you," Derek said. "How did you find us?"

Hendrix nodded at Sherlock. "That dog led the way. Once we got close enough, we held the dog back, just in case. But he brought us right to you."

Derek leaned down and rubbed Sherlock's fur.

"You're a good boy," he murmured.

"We've been trying to bust these guys for a long time," Hendrix said, nodding at Foxglove and Whitaker. "They're in a lot of trouble with the law."

"They were ready to kill us." Autumn shivered as she remembered how close to death they'd come.

Hendrix frowned. "You guys did well. You survived circumstances that most of us wouldn't have."

Autumn and Derek exchanged a look. The ranger only knew half of it, and it was going to take a while to run through the whole story with him. They'd have plenty of time for that later—once they were off this mountain.

"It was only because we worked as a team." Her gaze went to Derek.

As Hendrix wandered away to assess the scene, Autumn turned toward Derek.

"Thanks for your help out there," she told him. "I mean, we only survived because we worked together."

He shrugged. "I'm still sorry that I got you involved in all this."

"Like I told you before, you couldn't have known what your brother was up to."

"Smart thinking with Sherlock. I wasn't sure what you were doing, but I figured you had a plan. There was no way you would have just let Sherlock go otherwise."

She rubbed Sherlock's fur again. "He's never let me down yet."

Derek leaned toward her. "Autumn… I know this sounds crazy to say. I know we haven't known each other that long but—"

"I know," she filled in for him. "I feel it also."

"You do?"

She nodded. "Initially, I didn't want to feel anything. And when I realized I did, it scared me. I don't want to grow attached to someone, only to have something happen to them. I wasn't sure my heart could handle it."

Derek squeezed her hand. "I understand."

"But when I thought you were going to die out there in

the river… I knew without a doubt that I didn't want this to be the end for both of us." She wiped away the moisture that formed beneath her eyes.

A smile stretched across his face. "That makes me very happy to hear. I thought I'd messed things up."

She shook her head. "No, not at all. Once you've loved and lost someone…it makes you look at the future differently."

"I can only imagine." He leaned down and kissed her cheek. "I don't want to push you into something you're not ready for."

"I know without a doubt now that I am ready."

He grinned. "Good. Now…we need to have you checked out, especially that cut on your leg."

She bent her leg and felt the stiffness there. "It's true, but I think I'll be okay."

Derek raised an eyebrow. "After all of this settles, how about if we have dinner together?"

She grinned. "Dinner sounds really nice, especially if it's with you. Maybe even more than one."

"Definitely more than one."

The two of them shared a smile, and Autumn felt warmth spread through her chest. Spending more time with Derek was definitely an idea she could get used to. In fact, she could see herself enjoying his company for a long time.

TWENTY-FIVE

Six months later

Autumn looked up as she heard someone step onto her screened-in porch.

Her eyes lit with happiness when Derek came into view. He'd cleaned up really well. Actually, he'd looked great even when they'd been trapped in the wilderness.

But right now, his jaw was clean shaven, his hair neatly combed away from his face and he wore jeans with a short-sleeve top. Casual but professional. He looked very small-town lawyer.

Which was a good thing, since that's now what he was.

She hoped she looked better also. She was off work for the day but had donned some jeans and her favorite T-shirt. Her cuts and bruises had long since healed. Yet, in some ways, she'd always carry them with her. They reminded her of just how precious life was and how at the worst moments, God could send the biggest blessings.

Autumn stood to greet Derek, and he leaned toward her, planting a lingering kiss on her lips. Warmth spread through her at his nearness—just as it did every time they were close.

"Glad you made it," she said, leaving a hand on his chest.

"Time with you? I wouldn't miss it for anything."

The two of them shared a smile.

Then he leaned down and patted Sherlock on the head. The dog wagged his tail as he greeted him. Sherlock seemed to like Derek just as much as she did.

"Good to see you, boy," Derek murmured. "You've been taking care of Autumn for me?"

The dog barked in response.

As Derek and Autumn sat on the swing, Sherlock jumped up beside them and placed his front paws on Autumn's lap. The three of them fit perfectly.

"You got here just before the rain did," Autumn said, nodding outside.

She watched as the drops began to hit the leaves on the woods that surrounded her porch. They pitter-pattered on the tin roof above, and the pleasant scent of fresh rain filled the air. These were the kind of gentle storms she could handle, much more so than that awful line of storms that had trapped them on the mountainside last fall.

Gently, the swing undulated back and forth.

"I still can't believe you're here." She squeezed Derek's hand, never wanting to let go.

Not only had the two of them kept in touch with each other since their ordeal in the woods, but Derek had ultimately made the decision to take a job as prosecutor here in the county where Autumn was living. He just finished moving in this week.

Autumn had been anticipating seeing him all day today. At work, it had been all she was able to think about. She still couldn't believe he was really here. For good.

His arm slipped behind her, and she leaned into him, feeling totally relaxed.

"I could really get used to this," he murmured.

"I could get used to this, too. And, by this, I mean you being here with me."

He planted a kiss on her forehead before pulling her close again. "Me too. This was a good move."

"You're sure you don't miss DC and the fast-paced lifestyle there?"

"I don't miss it for a moment. I like the slower pace. But mostly I look forward to being with you...and Sherlock, of course."

The dog wagged his tail when he heard his name.

Autumn glanced down at the dog and rubbed his head again. Sherlock really had saved them that day. If he hadn't led the rangers into the woods, who knew what would have happened out there?

"I heard an update today on the case," she started.

"Did you?" Derek moved back just enough to see her face.

"Foxglove and Whitaker are going to be in jail for a very long time. We can definitely be thankful for that."

"That is good news," Derek said. "William is also getting the help that he needs. He's been in therapy, and he's trying to clean up his life, though there's still a chance that he might face some jail time."

"I'm glad to know that that whole situation might have a happy ending."

"Me too." Derek took in a breath and shifted. "In fact, there's something I want to ask you."

Autumn's heart thumped into her chest as she waited to hear what he had to say. She could hardly breathe. "What's that?"

"I know that we both had rocky roads to get here. But as soon as I met you, Autumn Mercer, I knew that you were different from anybody else I had ever talked to. I knew there was something really special about you."

He reached into his pocket and pulled something out. "That said, there's something I want to ask you."

Autumn sucked in a breath as she watched Derek get down on one knee.

Was this really happening? Was it possible that she could find true love twice in her life? It seemed too good to be true.

"Autumn, after Sarah left me at the altar... I didn't know if I ever wanted to look at forever again," Derek started. "I didn't think the heartache was worth it. Though our circumstances were different, I'm sure you can understand."

"I do."

"But when I met you, you brought something to life in me. When I imagined my future without you...it seemed grim."

She waited for him to continue.

"I realized I'd be a fool to ever let you walk away from me. I love you. Autumn Mercer, will you marry me?"

The air left her lungs. She didn't even have to think about her answer. "Yes, I will. I will marry you, Derek. I love you, too."

He slipped a beautiful engagement ring on her finger before rising to his feet. He pulled her along with him and tucked her closer. Their lips met.

As they did, Sherlock barked beside them.

They pulled away and chuckled. The dog jumped between them until he got a pat on the head.

Derek leaned toward the dog. "And yes, Sherlock, I want you to be a part of the family, too. Always."

The dog licked his face.

As Autumn watched all of it, her heart filled with

so much warmth and love that she'd never thought she would've been able to experience again.

But she was so grateful that things had worked out just the way that they were supposed to.

And now, against all odds, she was getting another chance at a happy-ever-after again.

* * * * *

Experience action-packed mystery and suspense in the K-9 Search and Rescue series:

Desert Rescue *by Lisa Phillips*
Trailing a Killer *by Carol J. Post*
Mountain Survival *by Christy Barritt*

If you enjoyed this exciting story of suspense and romance, pick up these other stories from Christy Barritt:

Hidden Agenda
Mountain Hideaway
Dark Harbor
Shadow of Suspicion
The Baby Assignment
The Cradle Conspiracy
Trained to Defend

Available now from Love Inspired Suspense!

Find more great reads at www.LoveInspired.com.

Dear Reader,

Thanks for reading Autumn, Derek and Sherlock's story.

Have you ever been in a situation similar to what they face in *Mountain Survival*?

Maybe your trial wasn't quite as dramatic. Maybe there weren't any floods or mudslides. Hopefully, there wasn't a potential killer chasing you. But we've all had times when we've felt like everything is working against us, when we feel like one storm comes right after the other.

Our comfort can be found in knowing these seasons only last for a period, and eventually blue skies return again. Keep your eyes up and have hope in the One who created the heavens and the earth.

Whatever part of your journey you're on, just know that we have a God who walks beside us every step of the way. Always.

Many blessings,

Get 4 FREE REWARDS!

We'll send you 2 FREE Books plus 2 FREE Mystery Gifts.

Love Inspired Suspense books showcase how courage and optimism unite in stories of faith and love in the face of danger.

FREE Value Over **$20**
